Carla

PATRICIA FRAME

ACKNOWLEDGMENT

My sincere thanks to my family, friends, teacher and classmates for their help, patience, and encouragement in completing this story. I truly appreciate all of you.

And a special thank you to my beloved, Bruce, whose support has been immeasurable.

CHAPTER ONE

Carla

Carla giggled and hopped back when the gentle ocean waves, rolling again and again over the sand, caught her bare toes. It had been a long time since she giggled, and it felt good.

Leaning against the corner of the arcade, Otra Vez's sheriff watched her as she played with the waves. "She doesn't belong here," he mumbled. Californians don't wear gray gabardine slacks with blue silk blouses to the ocean. And they certainly don't tie the sleeves of a cardigan sweater around their necks. Even a pretend Californian wouldn't be carrying black leather slippers. And her shoulder-length black hair just didn't fit his fun-in-the-sun beach. There hadn't been any serious trouble in his small town since he became sheriff, and he was not going to let any happen now.

Turning back to her car, Carla saw the sheriff watching her. Her heart started to pound. Taking a deep breath to calm down, she ordered herself not to jump to conclusions. Carla counted to three, smiled, and said to the sheriff, "Nice day you have here."

The sheriff nodded in agreement.

"Is there any place around here where I could get a decent meal?" she asked.

"The Seaside Diner is a few blocks that way," the sheriff said pointing toward the town.

Carla smiled in thanks and went to her car. She had just brushed the sand from her feet and settled down behind the steering wheel when a long black limousine drove slowly down the side street toward her. Quickly, she sunk down behind the wheel. The long limousine turned left and continued on out of town. "Silly girl," she told herself. But she knew it would not be hard to find her.

Carla had been driving for five weeks. Her brand-new green 1950 Ford two-door coupe now felt like part of her body. "You're crazy," her remaining friends told her when she left. "It's a dumb idea," they said. The more compassionate friend reminded her, "New York is only a phone call away. No reason not to stay in touch." But in reality, they had all stopped answering her calls.

Carla shook her head to chase the unhappy memories away. "This is what I need to do," she thought. "I'm 30 years old. I need to start over now. I need space where no one knows me or anything about me. This is not a mistake. Lord knows I made enough of those to recognize a new one." Looking west at the calm Pacific Ocean, she realized this was as far away from New York as she could get. Taking a deep breath, she slowly drove to the Seaside Diner.

Getting out of her 1950 Ford, she reached her arms over her head and stretched. She put her hands on her hips and leaned side to side. It felt good to be somewhere—although exactly where, she didn't know. The "Welcome to Otra Vez" sign didn't tell her much. Still, the ocean was calm, the beach was beautiful, and the mountains behind her made her feel protected. Maybe this would be a good place for her. She would soon find out.

The waitress behind the lunch counter watched Carla as she approached the diner and chose a booth next to the window where she could keep an eye on her car. "Have you named it?" the waitress asked.

Surprised, Carla turned her head and looked distrustfully at the waitress. "Named what?"

"Your car. Your license plate is from New York, so I figure you've been traveling a long time. Most people I know who travel a lot name their cars."

She turned to the side to get a better look at this waitress. Maybe this was not the place to stop. "I would like a grilled cheese sandwich," she said slowly while looking for other warning signs, like spinning eyes, or snakes poking out from her hair.

"Sure thing. Want something to drink with that?"

"I'll have a coke, and could you put tomato slices on the grilled cheese?"

"My favorite," the waitress said with a smile.

The window that Carla chose faced directly east. The Santa Lucia Mountains ringed the cove where this quaint little town was located. "I'm glad you're there," she silently told the mountains. "I don't want anything to do with what's behind you. You hide misery and hurt and lies." She paused. "Yes, there were happy times. But they ended in disaster. I'm glad to be gone."

"Here's your sandwich. Hope you enjoy it. My name is Wanda if you need anything else."

Carla ate her sandwich while she studied the placemat. "Otra Vez is a typical small town," she thought. "All the locals advertise on the diner's placemat." There was the real estate agent (always the largest ad), the local florist, the dentist, the medical clinic, and the auto mechanic. She stopped and looked closely at the last one. "Not every town this size has a foreign car mechanic. Must be some rich people here," she mused.

"Would you like dessert? We serve Bagonski's, the best pies in town," Wanda interrupted her thoughts.

"No, thanks. Say, can you tell me if there is a hotel in this town?"

"Oh, you mean you aren't visiting someone here?"

All of Carla's muscles tightened. She took a closer look at the waitress. Wanda was wearing a yellow dress and a small white apron adorned with a ruffle around the hem and a pocket holding a note-pad for taking orders—the usual waitress attire. Her hair was done up in a bun on top of her head with a yellow No. 2 pencil tucked into the bun. Her smile was soft and her eyes were a deep blue, like the ocean just a few blocks away. Carla judged her to be about the same age and could not see any signs of malice. Still, Carla thought Wanda's question was very rude. Keeping her voice steady, Carla replied, "No. Is there a hotel nearby?"

"Well, Mrs. Graham rents rooms over on Hill Street. She is a bit pricey though. There is the Ocean View Hotel down on Sea Side Boulevard. There are more motels along the Pacific Coast Highway, but they can be tricky to get in and out of."

"Thank you, uh, Wanda. May I please have my check now?"

"Sure." She handed Carla the check and, as she turned back to the counter, said, "If you need to know anything else, I'm usually here. I don't mean to be forward, but you do seem to be alone."

Carla glanced quickly around, hoping no one else heard. She didn't want everyone in town knowing her business. She relaxed. No worries. She was the only one there. "Thank you, Wanda. I just might take you up on that." She smiled and placed her money on the bill. Remembering her waitressing days, she added a nice tip.

Walking to her car, she glanced around, taking in the beautiful ocean view, the protective mountains on the north and south, the cliff on the east, and the small-town atmosphere. "This could be the place," she mused.

She drove past Mrs. Graham's boarding house. It looked pleasant enough, and tiny—probably only about six guests at a time. Carla's experience taught her small-group gossip spreads faster than wildfire. "Too risky," she mumbled and drove on down the block to the town park.

She pulled into a parking space, turned off the engine, and sat looking around. This was definitely not her New York. Boutique-style stores lined the streets facing the park. A statue stood in the middle of the park's two crisscrossing paths. Nothing stood between the statue and the ocean. The town had obviously been very strict with their zoning.

As she walked over to read the plaque on the statue, an old man sitting on a bench next to the path called out to her. "You're new here. Are you visiting or do you have enough sense to stay?"

Shocked, Carla stopped and looked him directly in the eye. "And just why should I stay?"

"Because this town suits you."

"What makes you think that?" Carla asked hesitantly.

"It's written on your face. Your face tells it all. You're running. Is it away from or to?" He watched her reaction closely.

She shifted from foot to foot, turned halfway, swung her shoulder bag from her left to her right shoulder, then looked back at him. She pulled her forehead slightly down, causing her lips to purse, and firmly stated, "To."

He nodded. "This is your place. I like you. You may ask me whatever you need to know." With that he picked up his newspaper and began reading.

Carla stood absolutely still. Did this really happen? She looked quickly to the left and right. No one was in sight. She looked back at the old man, or more accurately, his newspaper. She took four quick steps toward the Pacific, glanced back to make sure this wasn't a dream, then hurried toward the ocean. She was shaking.

"It's that plain. That obvious. I must stand out like a sore thumb. I have to make changes. I have to start my new life." Abruptly, she changed direction and made a beeline to the Clips & Curls shop across from the park statue. It was the beginning.

CHAPTER TWO

The Next Step

Gloria, the beautician, and Jessie, the shampoo girl, watched her walking toward them. "This one is going to be a no-win," Gloria stated. "She has an East Coast hairstyle."

"And East and West never meet," Jessie continued Gloria's thought.

The shop was empty when Carla entered. Looking at the three empty stylist chairs, she smiled and asked, "Is it possible for me to get my hair styled today?"

Gloria gave a quiet groan and sent a silent message to Jessie. "The place is empty. We do haircuts." Yep. This is a no-win for sure. Jessie spoke up, "I can do a shampoo first, if you like?"

Carla looked at Gloria. Gloria was squinting at Carla. "Do you have a style in mind?"

"Something different than what I have."

Gloria bit her bottom lip. "Yep," she thought, "I was right. This is going to be a no-win." Out loud she said, "I can give you a cut and blow dry. If that is what you want."

"Sounds perfect."

Jessie motioned to the shampoo chair. Carla smiled and walked over.

Gloria cut Carla's shiny black hair short—to the hairline in the back, swept up on the sides, with short bangs pushed to the left. She added some gel and brushed some gentle curls on top. It wasn't really necessary to blow dry the style. Gloria held up a mirror, then stepped back and waited for Carla to be outraged. "So this is California style?" Carla asked hesitantly.

"Easy-breezy, we call it."

Carla touched her hair and felt how much there wasn't. "Should be easy to take care of," she murmured. "It's going to take a bit to get used to it."

"You'll love it when you go to the ocean," Jessie tried to assure her.

"The ocean. Oh yes. Sure. How much do I owe you?" Carla paid the ladies, included a tip, and left the shop. She wasn't sure how the haircut looked, or how she looked, but it felt great. "A good beginning," she assured herself.

It wasn't much past two when she left the Clips & Curls shop and headed back to her Ford. She was about to cross over into the park when the display in the Corner Shop window caught her eye. She stopped and looked closer. The flowered Bermuda shorts and striped mid-calf-length pants made her giggle. No one in New York would wear those. "Why not?" she asked herself. "I'm making a change."

The clerks in the store were all too happy to help her pick out three pairs of shorts and two pairs of what they called "pedal push-ers," along with shirts that could be worn with either. They also sold her a pair of sneakers, telling her they were good for beach walking. She looked good in every outfit. Her body flattered clothes.

Since the sun was starting to drop toward the ocean, Carla decided to find a place to spend a night or two and headed to the Ocean View Hotel on Sea Side Boulevard. It was easy to find and just a short walk from the beach. After checking in, Carla tried on her new orange and green stripped pedal pushers and short-sleeve pull-over. The pullover was a soft orange jersey material with a boat neck-line. The low cut sneakers completed her outfit. She felt California beautiful. Too beautiful to stay indoors.

The sun was dropping lower, the night was still young, and the weather was balmy. Perfect for beach walking. She grabbed her keys and headed out. The view at the ocean's edge was more than just the wave after wave she expected. Some waves crashed on the shore, while others rolled gently in. Seagulls were rising and dipping along the shore. Fish were jumping out of the waves, and an ocean liner was headed to the horizon. Carla looked toward the town and saw that the evening sun sparkling on the windows looked like earthly stars. Trees waved gently along with the warm ocean breeze. Her eyes followed along the mountaintop ridge.

And there it was!

Setting in the center of the cliff that overlooked the cove was the most majestic house she had ever seen. The night sky was creep-ing up behind the adobe-colored house, making it look like pure gold. The setting sun was dancing on the six evenly spaced windows on the second floor. There appeared to be additions on the north and south sides. She couldn't be sure because the cliff edge hid the lower half of the house. "My California gold," she mumbled. "I found it! I want that house," she whispered. Granted, it probably needed work. It looked vacant. Some of the green window shutters were hanging down. "Minor problem," she told herself. "Tomorrow. Tomorrow I will find out all there is to know about my grand house." Holding her first finger and middle finger on her right hand together, she kissed them and touched her forehead. This oath to herself, she was determined to keep.

Carla ate a quick dinner in the hotel restaurant, hurried to her room, pulled a piece of paper from the desk, and began writing her plans. She barely slept that night.

CHAPTER THREE

The Plan

Carla needed to find the road to her dream house so she could check it out up close. Fortunately, common sense reared its head and told her not to make irrational decisions. See the place first. Don't let anyone know how much you want it or the price will double. It was sensible advice. But the butterflies in her stomach kept fluttering. She looked in the mirror at the California clothes she had chosen: green top and two tone green striped pedal pushers. "No one will mistake me for a rich person," she laughed.

She drove to the Seaside Diner. As she had hoped, Wanda was working. Only a few cars were in the parking lot, and they all had California license plates. "Probably all locals," she mumbled to herself. "I'll have to be careful who hears what I say."

Wanda saw her when she entered the diner. "Hi, I'm glad you're back. Want some coffee?"

"Yes, and pancakes if you have them."

"We only have the best in town," Wanda responded loudly. The other diners glanced at Wanda and Carla with surprised looks but said nothing.

While Carla sipped her coffee, the two diners sitting closest to her paid their bill and left. When Wanda brought her pancakes, Carla decided it was safe to ask. "Wanda, what can you tell me about the house on the cliff?"

"It's been vacant for a few years now." Wanda sat in the chair across from Carla and in a low voice she asked, "Did you see the ghost?"

"Ghost? I don't believe in ghosts. It just looks like an interesting house and I was wondering about its history."

"Oh. Well, it's very old. I think some gold miner struck it rich and built it."

"That's interesting," Carla was getting frustrated. "How do I get to it?"

"Oh you shouldn't go there. At least not by yourself. I've heard there are wild animals up there and they will chase you off the cliff."

"Who do you know that was chased off the cliff?"

"No one. But I was told it happens," Wanda said with a pouty voice. "It's been for sale for a long time. So maybe Sue at the real estate office could take you."

"Thanks, Wanda. You have stirred my curiosity even more. I'll tell Sue you sent me."

Carla paid her bill, including a tip, and started to her car. The beauty of the reflection of the sun on the ocean and its last morning rays shining on the mountains caused her to pause, but only momentarily. She was on a mission to see her house up close. It was only a few blocks to the real estate office and parking was not a problem. Parking never seemed to be a problem in Otra Vez.

Sue gave Carla the once-over when she walked in and decided she was a waste of time. Carla smiled at her, offered her hand, and said, "You must be Sue. Wanda sent me."

"Oh great," Sue thought. "One loser taking directions from another loser." Taking Carla's hand and putting on her business face, Sue said with her most syrupy voice, "I'm so glad to meet you. Please give my thanks and best to Wanda next time you see her. Now what can I do for you?"

"I'm interested in the house on the cliff."

"Oh, my dear. That house is very, very expensive. Besides it's much too large for one person. Let me show you the bungalow over on 2nd Street."

"I don't want a bungalow," Carla struggled to keep her voice steady.

"Well, I have a nice two-story colonial within walking distance. It is in your price range."

Carla clenched her teeth. She wanted to smack Sue. "How dare she judge me like that!" she thought to herself. "I have plenty of money. That crummy New York ex-boss, Winston, made sure of that. He told me he was buying out my contract. But, I knew it was really hush money, because no employment contract was worth what he paid me."

She could ruin his reputation, except what good would that do? Her reputation would also be ruined, and the victims would not be compensated. Besides, Winston did clean up his act some. At least, She was told he did.

"Sue, I have plenty of resources. If you don't want to show the house, just stay so. I understand there may be ghosts or dangerous animals running around the place. If you're scared, just say so."

Sue was taken aback. No one had ever spoken to her in such a manner. "I'm not scared!" she nearly shouted. "I'll get my keys. We can go now, if you want."

Carla smirked. It is simply too easy to shake some people. She waved her hand toward the door for Sue to lead the way. Once in the car, Sue began reciting facts about the house.

The central part of the dwelling was built in 1850. It sat on about twelve acres. A wing was added on the north side in about 1866. The wing on the south was added in the 1890s, before the Pacific Coast Highway was completed.

"Where is the Highway?" Carla asked.

"It runs close to the back of the property. There is a way in from there, but to my knowledge, no one uses it."

"Translation: She doesn't know where the property line is," Carla thought to herself. "Not to worry. The records at the courthouse will have all the details I'll need."

In less than a half hour, they were standing at the wrought-iron fence that rimmed the cliff and circled the house. Sue opened the gate and began describing the view of the town. "Down there, to the right of the courthouse, is the colonial I was telling you about. Over two streets to the left is the bungalow. You can see they have both been well-maintained; they even have fresh coats of paint."

Carla paid no attention to her. Her heart was racing as she looked at the grand stucco house. Running across the middle of the original house was a covered front porch at least thirty feet wide and twelve feet deep. The windows on the first floor were twice as tall as those on the second floor. And an oversized mahogany door with an etched-glass window was in the center of the porch. Thinking, "I don't care how run down it is. I want it," Carla opened her mouth to speak. Thankfully common sense took over again. "I want to see the inside." Sue heaved a sigh, nodded, and they headed to the front door.

The inside took Carla's breath away. The door opened onto a wide entrance hall with a marble floor, high ceilings, and hand-hewn corner cornices. There were archways on both sides of the entrance hall leading to the other rooms on the front of the original house. Running perpendicular to the entrance hall was a main hall with the same beautiful marble floor separating the front rooms from the back rooms. Straight ahead was an extraordinarily large window that began seven feet above the first floor and reached to just below the roof line on the second-floor rear wall. A U-shaped staircase began on the first floor to the right of the window, joined a landing that ran across the base of the window to its left side, and then turned and continued onto the second floor with ten more stairs. A wrought-iron railing with a music-scale-and-notes design lined the stairway. Carla was more sold than ever. She hurried over and ran her hand over the railing.

"Don't touch that," Sue scolded. "It might fall down. This is a very old house. Not like the bungalow, which has been well maintained."

"Let's look at the other rooms," Carla said, trying not to snarl. Opening onto the main hall to the left of the U-shaped stairway was a kitchen and two small rooms. To the right was a small room and a hallway leading to the back yard. Carla headed back to the entrance hall. She chose the archway on the north side to see first. It was a large room with high ceilings, crown moldings, and tall windows set deep in the walls. On the far side was a door that led to the northern addition. The walls of the addition were painted a bright red. The windows were tall, with stenciled gold markings around each one.

"That paint is going to be hard to cover," Sue said snidely.

"Those markings look like Chinese characters," Carla remarked.

"If they are, the Chinese will never be able to read them," Sue sneered.

Carla walked quickly to the room on the south side of the entrance hall. It was pretty much the same size as the north room, with high ceilings and matching tall windows. She hurried on to the south addition. It had the same high ceilings and tall windows, but the floor was amazing. Using different types of wood, the builder had created a starburst pattern. Carla gasped when she saw it. "That will take a lot of work to maintain," Sue said.

Carla returned to the main hallway, noting it extended to both the north and south, allowing each room in the original section to have two entrances. She returned to the U-shaped staircase and carefully climbed to the second floor, checking each step. It was solid. The four rooms on the front of the second floor were huge. Two more rooms were on the back, one on either side of the U-shaped stairway. All the rooms were much larger than they needed to be. "There are a lot of cracks in the plaster. And some of that tacky old wallpaper is peeling," Sue quipped.

Carla ignored her. She didn't really like the wallpaper anyway. They returned to the first floor and approached the back door. It was insignificant. Looking outside, Carla could see a lot of possibility for expansion. There was a large wooden structure that may have been a barn and an area that had definitely been a garden. The possibilities for this house were growing in Carla's mind. "What about the kitchen?" Carla asked.

"The previous owners started to remodel it. They left quite a mess. I'll show you if you really want to see."

"That's OK," Carla replied. At this point she figured she had antagonized Sue enough.

Returning to the front of the house, she estimated the distance to the cliff. Yes! The porch could be enclosed and still have room for a walkway to stroll and enjoy the beautiful ocean view. "Keep your cool, Carla. Keep your cool." The words ran incessantly through her mind. "Don't say too much. Don't give away too much."

"How much are they asking for this house?" she asked.

"$300,000," Sue replied. "And I don't think that is negotiable. The bank lost a lot of money on the previous owner."

"Really?" Carla did a good job hiding her delight at that bit of information. "What happened?"

"Well, a couple of fellows, just back from the war, decided they wanted to open a restaurant. So they bought this place and began remodeling it. They started to update the kitchen. Then, so I heard, they began arguing over additional costs. One left and the other couldn't meet the loan payments."

"A restaurant. Sounds like a very good idea."

"Well, not for them," Sue snarked.

"So the bank is the owner," Carla finished her statement. Carla had worked in finance in New York. She had seen how easy it was to prey on borrowers, especially ones with dreams. Give them a loan at a high interest rate, sell the loan for a lower rate and pocket the difference, collect unnecessary fees that go straight to the lender's pocket, loan more than they can afford, then foreclose. She saw people beg for more time and witnessed their despair when it all collapsed.

Her next step became clear. Tomorrow she would go to the bank. She would wear her California pedal pushers, and she would say all the right things to the banker. They'd never know what hit them. She smiled to herself.

"Ready to go?" Sue asked. "I'm sorry to have wasted your time. Let me show you the colonial."

"No thanks." Carla kept her voice steady. "I think I want to go back to the hotel."

During the entire trip back, Sue continued telling the history of the little town, including names of important people and who was related to whom. Carla listened intently. She knew this was going to be important to her future.

CHAPTER FOUR

The Deal

After saying a polite goodbye to Sue, Carla hurried to the courthouse. Even though it was past lunchtime, she didn't care. Getting the information on the loan against the house was much more important than food.

Carla knew her way around property and loan records. She had seen how lenders could turn an undesirable loan into a handsome commission. "I better not tip my plan to anyone here," she reminded herself. "If I do, the bank will know before I do."

The clerk smiled at her and asked how she could help her. Carla smiled back and in a soft voice inquired where she might find the listing of property loans. The clerk gave her a quizzical look. In a low voice, Carla explained, "I heard there were some foreclosures and I might be able to get a good deal on a house. Is that true?"

The skeptical clerk wasn't sure how to answer. If this girl standing in front of her dressed in pedal pushers and tennis shoes was as dumb as she looked, what would be the harm in letting her see the records? Besides, the records were open to the public anyway. "The property records are in that room over there." She pointed to the right. "The list of open foreclosures is on the last shelf and listed by street address. There aren't many. We are a small town."

Carla thanked her profusely, causing the clerk to shy away from her and bury her head in non-work. Carla hurried to the next room and easily found the bank note for her dream house. The original amount was for $200,000, of which $50,000 had been paid. It had been in default for two years. The names on the loan were Dirk C. Jenkins and Phillip W. Bagonski. "What a strange partnership," she mused. "Bagonski, Bagonski. Why does that name sound so familiar?"

Satisfied she had all the information she needed, she returned to the clerk's desk. "Thank you so much," she gushed.

The clerk nodded. "Did you find what you were looking for?"

"Not exactly," she half-lied and headed to the door. Across the street the old man was standing next to his bench watching her. A shiver ran down her spine. She hurried to her car and drove back to the hotel. She needed to prepare for her meeting at the bank tomorrow. But tonight she would take a walk on the beach and maybe, just maybe, gather a bit more information.

It was a particularly beautiful night. The sun, hanging barely above the horizon, was about to spread its beautiful pinkish-orange colors to the north and to the south. Shades of night were creeping from the east over the cliff. "There she is!" someone screamed. Everyone, including Carla, turned toward the cliff. A wispy figure was floating along the edge of the cliff. "It's the Captain's wife," a beautiful girl whispered. "No. It's the Prospector's dance hall girl," said a hunky fellow in a red bathing suit. "You would know," snarled the girl by his side. And then the wispy figure was gone. Carla said nothing. She knew it was the shadow cast by a seagull gliding high along the ocean's edge.

Sea Captain, Prospector, ghost—it all sounded like free publicity to Carla, not to mention a reason to lower the price. Not many people want to buy a house with that kind of history. But they will pay good money to visit. Her plan was coming together.

Back at the hotel, she stopped in the restaurant for a bite to eat before signing off for the night. As she finished her hamburger and fries, the young waiter came to her table with the dessert menu. "You should try the apple turnovers. They're the best in town."

"How do you know?" Carla teased.

"Because they're from Bagonski's." He stood straighter when he said that.

Carla recognized the name. "Are you a Bagonski?" she asked.

"I wish," he lamented. "I only go to school there. I'm studying to be a chef."

Carla's ears perked up. She was going to need a chef, and interns were cheaper than fully accredited chefs. "Did the owner of your school once own the house on the cliff?"

The waiter shifted his weight to his left foot. "We don't talk about that," he mumbled, before steering the conversation back to the dessert menu. "We make really good pies, too. Would you prefer that?"

"I'll take the turnover." Carla knew when to drop a sensitive subject. Besides, if the turnover was any good, she might have a lead for another part of her plan.

The turnover was indeed delicious. The crust was flaky and the apples were soft, the way Carla liked them. She paid her bill, left a nice tip, and went to her room. It had been a good day.

CHAPTER FIVE

Negotiating

The apple turnover gave Carla an idea that kept her up most of the night. She rose early the next morning. Her conversation with the young waiter convinced her the Phillip W. Bagonski listed on the foreclosure form had a connection to the Bagonski Culinary School. The bank opens at ten. Most schools open at seven or eight. "I can make both places easily. And the more information I have, the better for me."

Carla put on a soft orchid-colored silk blouse and a gray pleated skirt. "This town is small. The school will be easy to find. I will have to be careful who I ask so the banker doesn't get tipped off," she reminded herself. Looking in the mirror, she frowned. She needed more panache. Carefully she added the opal pendant surrounded by tiny diamonds her ex-boss, Winston, had given her. Gritting her teeth, she pulled on nylons, making sure the seam ran straight up the back of her leg. "The pedal pushers would be much more comfortable," she sighed. "I have to make a strong appearance," she scolded herself, squeezing into dress shoes with three-inch high heels. She groaned and switched to sandals.

The front desk had a map of the town with all the hotspots noted. Her dream house was not one of them. The culinary school was slightly to the south of town. Since the bank was on the opposite north side, there would be less chance of anyone seeing her and reporting to the bank. She couldn't help but smile. Things were going her way. She rushed out the front door to her car, pausing a brief moment before opening the car door. The sun was not yet high in the sky. The breeze from the ocean smelled sweet and fresh, and it seemed to be telling her this was the best decision she had ever made.

The culinary school was easy to find. The students wearing white chef jackets were scurrying from their cars to their classes. She followed them into the building, stopping and savoring the aromas of the fresh-baked bread. "I would weigh two tons if I worked here," she thought.

After noting the names of the staff listed on the directory by the front door, she was convinced she was right. Phillip W. Bagonski, Director, was at the top. She quickly found her way to the administrative offices.

Carla entered the front office. There was a wooden counter stretching halfway across the room, and three secretary desks were behind that. A box of fresh chocolate iced donuts sat enticingly on the end of the wooden counter. Across the side wall was a copier and bookshelves filled with three-ring binders. The receptionist behind the counter greeted her warmly. "Welcome. How may I help you?"

"My name is Carla DuPree. I would like to speak with Mr. Bagonski."

"Is he expecting you?"

"No. But it is very important I speak with him now. He will understand once I have a word with him." The receptionist hesitated. Carla smiled and begged, "Please." The receptionist went to one of the secretaries who looked up and studied Carla. "Oh no," Carla worried, "What if she has heard about me? Sue could have said something. Who could she have called?" The secretary rose, slowly walked to the door labeled "Director," and cautiously knocked on the solid wood door.

"Yes," said a voice from behind the door. The secretary entered, closing the door behind her. The receptionist smiled. Carla smiled back. After a few very long minutes, the secretary returned and ushered Carla into Phillip's office.

Rising from his high-back office chair, Phillip offered his hand to Carla while memorizing every inch of her from head to toe: the orchid-colored silk blouse, the gray pleated skirt, the pendant hanging down to the second button on her shirt. "Please have a seat," he said politely and motioned to the chair on the opposite side of his desk.

Carla shook his hand and sat down. She began, "I will only take a short amount of your time, and if you don't want to tell me, please say so. You are the Phillip Bagonski that began remodeling the cliff house, are you not?"

"That is correct." He leaned back in his chair and crossed his suntanned muscular arms across his culinary school T-shirt. The lemon tree lesson sounded loudly in his head: "The lemon tree is very pretty, but the fruit is impossible to eat." He was not going to be taken in by beauty.

Carla took a deep breath. "I am on my way to the bank. I want to buy that house. I was hoping you could tell me, or I should say, warn me about it. Is the plumbing in good shape? How about the electric? Do you know about anything structural that may need repair? How about the roof?"

"Slow down. I don't know who you are or who you represent. Or even what you plan on doing with that old place. Why should I give you any information? What's in it for me?" He leaned forward, resting his clasped hands on the desk.

"I'm sorry. I'm very excited and pretty nervous." Carla squirmed in her chair.

"Well you better get over that before you talk to the bank. They are not happy with the loss they are holding on that place. No one has made an offer on it in the two years since they foreclosed, and I couldn't find a buyer or another partner before that. And I don't want one now. I'm completely tied up with my school."

"I'm in this by myself. I want to develop a resort with a theater, overnight rooms, and a restaurant. Maybe some gardens. I'm still in the planning stage. I need to see what is there before I can actually decide."

Phillip leaned back, his blond hair glowing in the sun peeking through the window. He asked again, "What's in it for me?"

"I had one of your apple turnovers last night and it was delicious."

Phillip shrugged his shoulders, "Of course."

"If that is how good your students cook, I would hire them as interns at my restaurant. It would add to your already impressive school. And I would pay you a finder's fee for each intern. And, if you are willing, I will hire you as a consultant for my restaurant." Carla felt her confidence grow when she came up with such a good deal.

Phillip smiled. He liked her spunk. Rising to his full six feet, he moved directly in front of her and leaned back against his desk. His T-shirt was pulled taut over his muscular chest and thin waist. His thighs pressed against the thin cotton of his chef's pants. Carla struggled to maintain her professional persona.

Phillip looked at the floor, then back at Carla. "The house is in good shape. The last I was there, the roof was fine. The plumbing worked too, but it should be checked anyway because of not being used. The house mostly needs cleaning and cosmetic updates. And you will need a parking lot. The grounds around the house also need a lot of work. That old iron fence won't keep anything from falling."

"Not even the ghost?" Carla chuckled.

"No fence can stop a ghost," Phillip shot back. Carla didn't know if he was kidding or not. Phillip paused for a moment, then asked, "How much is the bank asking?"

"$300,000."

"That's too much. Even if the place was in perfect shape, getting there is not easy."

"What about the Pacific Coast Highway? Sue at the real estate office said it ran close to the back of the property."

"Sue is an idiot. I was told some land up there is tied up with the National Park Service. I'm not sure exactly where. Look, the bank has already recouped $50,000 on the $200,000 loan, plus all the interest I paid. They loaned us more than the place was worth then and now. Don't pay a penny more than the loan balance. And if you can, pay less."

Carla stood to leave and reached out her hand to Phillip. He wrapped both his hands around hers, quickly checking for rings. She did the same. "Thank you," Carla said and turned toward the door.

As she reached for the doorknob, Phillip said, "Lose the sandals. And let me know how it goes at the bank."

Carla smiled, "You'll be the first." Why not? She didn't know anyone else who cared.

Phillip stood at his office door watching her leave. Carla hesitated as she passed the box of donuts. "Go ahead. Help yourself to what you want," Phillip said with a crooked smile.

Carla blushed and said, "Some other time." Phillip snickered.

"Pretty girl," his secretary said after Carla was out the door.

"Sure is," Phillip agreed. "She wants to buy the cliff house."

"Aren't you going to stop her?"

"Why should I?"

"Aren't you letting her walk into a disaster?"

"She has to get past the bank first. She's alone. If she fails, I'll be happy to help her get over it," Phillip chuckled.

"You should be ashamed of yourself," the secretary scolded softly. "My money says she gets it. I'll even bet you fifty cents."

CHAPTER SIX

The Bank

Carla's hotel was between the culinary school and the bank. It was only ten in the morning. The bank was a short fifteen minutes away. Having skipped breakfast, and passing up the donut, she was now feeling hungry. She decided to get a bite to eat at the hotel restaurant while retrieving her three-inch high heels. When ordering a large cup of coffee and a cherry Danish, she asked the waiter, "Is the Danish from the Bagonski Culinary School?"

"Yes, ma'am."

She tried to eat the Danish slowly so as not to aggravate her already nervous stomach, but it was just too good. The light-brown crust with perfectly arranged cherry filling not only tasted good, it was a feast for the eyes. "This alone could make my restaurant a success," she mused. Sitting at the table, she pulled her notepad out of her leather briefcase and reviewed her notes.

Original loan over value of property.

Received 25 percent of original loan plus interest with payments and some later—not sure how much.

Interest rate was higher than average at the loan date.

Would not bargain with borrower.

House is approximately one hundred years old.

Inside needs cosmetic work, maybe plumbing.

Outside needs minor work.

Landscaping needs major work, including a new fence and parking lot.

Land use may be limited due to National Park Service.

Town says it has a ghost.

Closing her notebook and giving it a determined thump, she encouraged herself, "I've got this."

She arrived at the bank at ten thirty, precisely what she had calculated as the perfect time. The morning rush of problems would be taken care of and the staff would have settled down into their humdrum routines. Taking a deep breath and holding her head high, she opened the door and walked in. All heads turned. Mr. Cohen— bank manager, according to his desk nameplate—came to attention. Carla was different than the usual bank customer. She wore three-inch heels and stockings with the seams straight up the back of her well-formed calves, and she walked with confidence. But she had a California short haircut. He would have to be careful dealing with her.

Glancing around, Carla quickly determined that Mr. Cohen was the only one who could help her. She walked confidently toward him with a smile on her face. Reaching out her hand, she asked, "Mr. Cohen?"

"Yes. May I help you?" He was unnerved, and it showed.

"I am here to buy the cliff house," she informed him. "I will pay you $100,000 in cash."

Money always brought Mr. Cohen back to his senses. "The property is for sale for $300,000," he responded.

"Mr. Cohen, we both know the property is not worth $300,000. It was not even worth the $200,000 you loaned the previous owners when you gave them the loan, and certainly not now. Add that to the fact the house has been empty for two years, causing further deterioration, and I believe $100,000 is more than a fair valuation."

"It seems you have done some homework on this site. Who do you represent on this purchase?"

"Myself."

Mr. Cohen was skeptical. "It's a very big house for one person."

"I intend to turn it into a retreat, starting with a restaurant."

"I'm not sure the town zoning will allow that," he tried stalling for time.

"It must, because you already loaned money to build a restaurant there. And a retreat will draw people to the town, where they will want to shop and enjoy the beach. It will be very good for the town." Her point was not wasted. It doesn't pay for a banker in a small town to upset the business owners.

"You have obviously researched the property carefully. Therefore, you know the amount outstanding on the loan is $150,000. I can't possibly accept any amount less than $175,000 to cover back taxes and other lost revenue."

Carla pulled her pad from her briefcase and began listing items that might require additional funds. Plumbing: $5,000. Plaster and flooring: $6,500. Fence: $2,500. Roof: $10,000. Shutters: $1,000. She slanted the paper so he could see without obviously looking. She added, Parking lot: $2,000.

Mr. Cohen leaned back and rubbed his chin. He knew what she was doing. "The plumbing and roof are fine."

"That was two years ago. Time takes a toll. Your bank has recouped 25 percent of the initial loan plus interest at a higher than average rate. The bank's working capital is tied up in an uncollectible loan and losing at least 5 percent interest every day. No one else has even looked at the property, let alone made an offer. And then there is the ghost."

Mr. Cohen's face went blank. Carla was not a head-in-the-sky dreamer. She knew her stuff.

Carla reached over and picked up Mr. Cohen's business card. She ran her finger over the words, hesitating at the "Branch Office" designation. The action was not lost on Mr. Cohen.

"Give me till tomorrow afternoon. I will see if the bank will accept $165,000."

"Mr. Cohen," Carla said in her best business voice, "The loan originated at this office; you signed it. You foreclosed on it. You have the power to accept or reject any offer regarding it. I can pay you $140,000 right now."

Mr. Cohen put his hands together intertwining his fingers and raised them to his mouth. "Where's the money?"

"In a bank in New York. I can have it wired in twenty-four hours."

Now he understood. He was right. She was not the run-of-the-mill girl with a dream. Still, he didn't want to take any chances on her bringing in an undesirable element. "Where did you get that kind of money?" As soon as the words were out of his mouth, he regretted saying them.

Carla bristled. He shouldn't have asked that and he knew it. Now it was too late. Now she could either take advantage of his slip of the tongue or play the "let's be nice" card. Knowing that when, not if, she got the house, she would probably be dealing with him on other matters, she chose the "let's be nice" card. "It's in a trust fund set up for me by my parents. They died a couple of years ago." There was no reason to tell him where all her money came from.

"$140,000 it is. You make the arrangements for the money transfer and I'll have the papers drawn up. Can you meet tomorrow afternoon at two?" He did not look happy, but he did look relieved.

"Yes. And of course, I will need to establish a bank account with this office. See? You are already recouping lost money."

Mr. Cohen gave a slight smile. They shook hands and Carla left. The old man in the park was watching. He gave her a thumbs up. She quickly looked away.

CHAPTER SEVEN

Next Step

Ownership of the house was so close, Carla could taste it. She walked slowly through the park. She wanted to run. She wanted to skip. But now was not the time. Right now she had to maintain her professional aura.

By the time she reached her hotel, she was ready to burst. "Not yet," she told herself. "First I have to get the money wired." That should not be a problem. She had discussed the possibility with Ron before she left. Ron Gunderson was her financial advisor and confidant. She checked the time. New York was three hours later than California. It would be the end of the day there. She better hurry.

She had all her account numbers, balance, and amount to be wired at her fingertips. She dialed Ron's office number and took deep breaths while she waited for an answer. It only took four rings, but it seemed like all day. "Mr. Gunderson's office. May I help you?" said a reassuring New York voice.

"May I please speak with Mr. Gunderson? This is Carla DuPree."

"One moment please."

"Carla! How are you? Ready to come home yet? We miss you back here." Ron Gunderson's voice sounded sincere. Ron had watched Carla grow up. She was the flower girl at his wedding. He had been the custodian of her trust fund set up by her parents from the beginning. Once she was of legal age, he began dealing directly with her and they became good friends.

"No. I'm still on the run," Carla laughed. Ron laughed with her.

"What can I do for you Carla? Or should I say how much money do you need?"

"You know me too well. I need $140,000 wired tomorrow. I found a business opportunity too good to lose." There was a moment of silence on the other end. "Are you still there Ron?"

"Yes. I think it best if I fly out and help you close the deal. It might be quicker than wiring the money." Ron was stalling. He couldn't keep from being protective of Carla. He knew she had been stung before, so she was now not as innocent as she had been in the past. Still, business is a man's world, and he didn't want anyone taking advantage of her again.

"Ron, I must do this myself. I'm at the bottom. You know that. If I can pull this off, there'll be no stopping me. I need to get back where I was. Please understand." Carla was begging. Ron began to soften.

"What kind of business is it?" He was still stalling.

"It's an old mansion that I want to turn into a retreat of sorts. It sets on top of a cliff and has a beautiful view of the ocean. There is access from the east and west. I plan on starting with a restaurant then adding rooms for conferences and overnight stays. I already have a chef lined up. Please trust me on this one, Ron. Once it is mine, I'll send you pictures."

"What's the total price? Are you borrowing from someone or are you taking on a partner?"

"The total price is $140,000. It will need some updating and repairs. I estimate another $50,000. I plan on doing the add-ons as profits permit."

"You sound like your old self, Carla. Still, I am hesitant."

"Don't be. I learned my lesson."

"Give me the numbers. I'll wire the money at noon tomorrow."

"Perfect! Love you bunches. Watch for the pictures!" Carla hung up the phone and did a little dance in her hotel room. Ron slowly put the phone down and worried. It was her money. He really had no control. Yet, he worried.

Carla ate at the hotel restaurant and walked to the beach. She chose a lounge chair facing the ocean and turned it to face the cliff. She sat there for an hour admiring her house. She wanted to call Phillip, but the deal wasn't finalized yet and she didn't want to take a chance on jinxing it.

The last rays of the sunset were barely peeking over the western horizon when Carla began to stir from her observation position. As she leaned forward, a hand touched her shoulder. "I thought you were going to call me when you owned the house?" Carla jumped at the touch. It was Phillip. "Sorry, I didn't mean to scare you. But you didn't call me."

"It's not mine yet," Carla stammered. "How did you know?"

"It's a small town, Carla. Everyone knows. How about going to the Golden Surf to celebrate?"

"Oh, sorry. I already had dinner. Besides, the deal isn't signed yet."

"Carla DuPree. Are you, the girl from New York, superstitious?" Phillip chuckled.

"Why did you say 'the girl from New York'?" Carla asked suspiciously.

"Your license plate. Everyone has seen it. That's why they all call you the girl from New York."

"People talk about me?" Carla was a bit taken aback. She didn't know if this was good or bad. "I guess I better get my license changed. Anyway, I'm not superstitious. But, on the outside chance there are ghosts, I wouldn't want to upset any of them. So, I think it's wise to play it safe," Carla laughed.

"Then how about a cup of coffee at the diner?"

"Sounds good to me."

They walked to Phillip's car and drove to the Seaside Diner. Wanda was working. Wanda was always working, it seemed.

"Congratulations!" Wanda called as they entered the diner.

Carla was taken aback. "You, too?" she asked.

"It's a small town, Carla. Everyone knows," Wanda smiled.

On the drive back to her hotel, Carla noticed her cliff house could not be seen at night. "I'll fix that!" she promised herself. "Maybe I'll put a lighted statue of the ghost up there," she chuckled to herself.

"What's funny?" Phillip asked.

"Can't tell you yet!" she giggled.

CHAPTER EIGHT

The Closing

Carla woke early. Her excitement was overflowing. Her head was spinning with ideas for her new adventure and possible problems for the same. It was too early in California to do anything, but it was the right time in New York. Carla called Ron to make sure the money was wired. It was. Ron offered again to come for the closing. Again, Carla refused his help.

Looking out her hotel window, she noticed traffic was picking up. People were heading to work, and it dawned on her—in a few hours she would be joining them. "I am going to be one of them! I am going to be part of this community. I will no longer be the 'girl from New York.'" A slight smile crossed her lips. She couldn't help it. Being a "part" felt good. She hurried to the closet and pulled out a flowered sundress with short sleeves and a scooped neckline. "Perfect!" She slipped into her sandals and fluffed her easy-breezy hairstyle. Standing in front of the mirror, she spun around, making the sundress' skirt swirl out. Giving herself two thumbs up, she headed to the door.

Carla hurried out of the hotel and jumped into her car. She wanted to talk to the old man on the bench. She circled the park looking for him. He was there. Right on the bench by the statue. A parking space was barely ten feet away from him. There was always lots of parking. She turned the key off and hesitated. Maybe this wasn't a good idea. She didn't know his name. She never saw anyone speaking to him. Still, he had spoken to her. He had been watching her. Although it seemed creepy, she didn't really feel any fear of him. He wasn't a big man, only five foot seven or eight. He was probably skinny, she couldn't be sure because of the way he always dressed in button shirts, usually plaid, and heavy work pants. His shoes had steel-toes that were not scuffed enough to be used for work. He was always clean and his hair was combed. Still, he looked a bit disheveled. She walked boldly toward him. He lowered his newspaper and stared at her with a blank face.

"Otra Vez," she said. "The name of this town, Otra Vez, translates into *another time*. Does it mean 'go away and come another time,' or 'try again'?" The old man's expression did not change. "The first time you spoke to me, you said I was running, and that this town suited me. Did you mean I should try again, Otra Vez?"

The old man squinted one eye, pulling his face into a half grin. "Go get something to eat. You need to calm down before your meeting with the bank. And, oh, don't drink any more coffee. You're on edge enough." He returned to his newspaper, thus dismissing Carla.

"You're a frustrating old man," she scolded. He made no motion or response. Carla walked to the edge of the beach and bought an egg salad sandwich and a bottle of caffeine-free root beer.

At 1:45 she walked into the bank for her two o'clock meeting with Mr. Cohen. All eyes turned when she entered. Mr. Cohen reached out his hand to her. Gawking at her perfectly fitted flowered sundress and sandals, he gushed, "I see you have become one of us." Getting his wits back, he continued, "I have the papers right here. The money arrived just as the bank was opening. Thank you for being so prompt."

Carla smiled and shook his hand. "I am beginning to feel at home here. I'm sure as soon as I have the key to the cliff house in my hand, I'll start speaking your language." They both gave a nervous laugh. The rest of the meeting went off without further ado. When Mr. Cohen handed Carla the key, she waved it in the air and shouted, "Woohoo!" All the employees in the bank waved back, clapped, and shouted, "Woohoo," surprising her. Carla smiled and hurried to the door. She was going to meet Phillip. He was going to take her to her new house on the cliff. Life was great. The old man kept his newspaper in front of his face so no one could see his tears, tears of joy.

CHAPTER NINE

It's Mine

Phillip was waiting at the hotel when Carla arrived. She jumped out of her car and waved the cliff house key in the air. "It's mine. It's mine," she shouted. Phillip laughed.

"Well then, what are we waiting for? I have champagne and caviar already packed in my car. Let's go." Phillip made a cavalier sweep with his arm and held the door open for her. Carla laughed and hurried over. She was on her way to her dream.

"The sky is perfect. The ocean is perfect. Otra Vez is the perfect little town and the perfect slogan for me," Carla gushed.

"The perfect slogan?" Phillip repeated.

"Yes. Otra Vez. Another time. This is another time for me and this time it's the right time. I can feel it. This time I am doing everything right. This time, I will be successful for me. Oh, I wish Mom and Dad could be here. They tried to warn me before. They told me others were taking advantage of me. I couldn't see it then, but I can now." She turned toward Phillip, "I will never treat others that way."

"Where are your folks?" Phillip asked, thinking that was the safest topic to discuss while driving.

"They died a few years ago."

"I'm sorry. They must have been young. Was there an accident?"

"Oh, no. They weren't young. They adopted me when they were in their forties. Oh look! I can see my wrought-iron fence." Carla waved her arm in front of Phillip's face, nearly blocking his view of the road.

Phillip pulled through the gate and up close to the house. Carla jumped out and ran to the wide wooden stairs leading to the front porch of her large, very large, adobe-colored stucco house. Phillip was right behind her. At the top of the stairs, she turned and admired the ocean view. "Yes," she whispered, and stomped across the porch to the north end, turned and stomped to the south end. Smiling, she turned to Phillip, "It's sturdy. I will be able to serve guests out here." Not waiting for an answer, she pulled out the key and faced the door.

Phillip put his hand over hers to stop her shaking so the key would go into the lock. Carla chuckled. The door opened and the exquisite marble floor of the entrance hall greeted them. "It's beautiful," Carla said.

"It needs a good cleaning," Phillip replied. Carla ignored him. They entered the large room on the north side through the archway on the left side of the entrance hall.

"I will be able to serve about forty people in here," Carla said, not noticing the peeling paint.

"More than that," Phillip acknowledged quietly. He was remembering all the estimates and plans he and Dirk had made before they lost the cliff house. He shook his shoulders trying to ward off his sadness. This was Carla's day. He was determined not to spoil it. "Come, let me show you around the kitchen." He took her hand and led her through the paneled door to the kitchen.

Carla didn't even peek at the kitchen during the walk-through. Now that she was seeing it, she was convinced she made a very smart deal. It looked like a kitchen on a major ship. A stainless steel stove with three ovens was in place. An empty space was still waiting for a double refrigerator. "You don't have much to finish here," Phillip said almost apologetically.

"Will you help me?" Carla said with a pleading voice. She was beginning to realize she didn't know everything she needed to know.

"Of course," he replied without thinking how this would affect him. He thought he was over his restaurant dream. Now he wasn't so sure. To stop the doubts, he suggested, "Let's survey the rest of your dream."

Leaving the kitchen, they turned and entered the northern addition. "It is believed this was added by the Sea Captain because he traded in goods from China. Some of the trim features Chinese characters."

"Probably happy thoughts since this was his home, I hope," Carla said.

Continuing their tour, Carla noted the front room on the south side would be good for banquets, and the addition on the south side with the starburst parquet floor would be good for dancing. Entering the south addition, Carla held her arms out to the side and began dancing around the room. When she danced by Phillip, she held her arms out toward him and they waltzed around the room holding each other at arm's-length. Finally, out of breath, she asked, "Who made this starburst pattern on the floor?"

"I think it was the naturalist that lived here. Anderson or Johnson or something like that. He used maple, redwood, cherry, and mahogany woods. It was rumored he was friends with Roosevelt and Muir. They say one time, Muir and Emerson visited here. It had something to do with the redwoods and Yosemite. You know there are some redwood trees on the back of this property."

"You mentioned that before. I will need to do some research about it. I don't want to get in trouble with the National Park Service."

"Bad publicity?"

"You know it." They continued their inspection of the second floor, pausing on the landing to admire the view of sky and trees through the exceptionally big window.

"Do the trees make you homesick for back East?" Phillip asked softly, hoping to learn a little more about her.

"No," she answered. "I lived in the city. Trees are scarce there."

Turning right, they entered a room on the back of the house above the kitchen. Shyly Phillip told Carla, "We stayed here while we were working on the place. We didn't do any rehab up here."

"Obviously," Carla agreed.

They came back down the open staircase, checking the view from each step as they descended to the main hallway. The oversized back door was to the south of the staircase.

Envisioning the traffic flow, Carla suggested the back door may be the best entrance and began checking it out. The short hallway to the door was adequate. The door opened out onto a large flat grassy area where the one-time garden was obvious. The barn-like structure was about one hundred feet off to the left, and what looked like a driveway ran from there into the woods on the back of the property. She hadn't noticed the driveway at the walk-through with Sue. She began quizzing Phillip: "Is that a driveway? Where does it go? Did you use the barn?" Carla was full of questions.

"We never got around to really looking at the barn. The driveway leads to another road that connects to the Pacific Coast Highway. We always came up through Otra Vez. You definitely need a gardener. How about some champagne?" Showing the house to Carla brought back memories he didn't expect, and some were hard to bear.

The sun was beginning to set. The beautiful pink and orange colors of the Pacific sunsets always made Carla feel peaceful. It would be a wonderful end to this exciting day. "That would be perfect," she said.

They sat on the front porch watching the sunset, eating caviar, and drinking champagne, both lost in their own thoughts, while the radio softly played love songs. Carla's thoughts drifted toward romance. She tilted her head. Looking up at Phillip she whispered, "This is nice. I feel relaxed and ready for," she paused, "anything."

Phillip looked down at her smiling face, her sparkling eyes, her easy-breezy haircut. His heart was racing. Should he take a chance? Was she really ready for anything? The girls in his office told him to strike while the iron was hot. But how was he to know? The other girls he had dated were all over him by this time. Carla wasn't. She was different from those girls. She could actually carry on an interesting conversation. And what if "anything" didn't include what he wanted, what his body was screaming for? He swallowed hard and said, "Good to know. Want some more champagne?"

Carla was a little disappointed in Phillip's response. Too soon, she reasoned and held her glass out. Work could wait till tomorrow. Tonight was for simply enjoying her newfound life.

CHAPTER TEN

The Beginning

Sleep came hard the first night of ownership. But when it came, it was deep and restful. Carla woke in her hotel room full of energy and excitement. This was her Otra Vez, her new start. She began clicking off in her mind what she needed to do: Make arrangements for two telephone lines, one personal, one business; check on the electric service; find a carpenter, cleaning people, and a landscaper; find a bed and table so she could eat and sleep in her magnificent new house.

The phone lines were taken care of with a phone call from her hotel room. They would be connected in two days. She needed to go to the Otra Vez Utilities Office to have the electric transferred to her name. "Be sure to bring your sales contract for proof," the congenial clerk reminded her, and then added, "We're glad you moved here." Carla was surprised. She had never experienced such friendly service.

She was sure she could get the names of some carpenters and cleaning people at the hardware store. Finding a landscaper was going to be a bit trickier. That left only the bed and table to take care of. But everything was falling into place so easily that Carla wasn't worried.

Knowing she would be using the bed and table for years, Carla decided to treat herself and get really good furniture. After checking for messages at the hotel's front desk, Carla drove to the only furniture store in Otra Vez. The store had quite a selection, but nothing that appealed to Carla.

"Can I help you?" the well-dressed salesman asked.

"I hope so. I need a good strong bed as soon as possible." Carla said, glancing past him at the Danish-style furniture.

The salesman bristled. "How soon?" he asked, cautiously trying to decide if he wanted her for a customer. "You can rent a room down the street if you are in a hurry to sleep." He looked her up and down with judgmental eyes.

Appalled, Carla's eyes narrowed. Her shoulders dropped. She thought, "This place is just as sexist as New York." But not wanting to take a chance on losing even one customer, she pulled her shoulders back in place and began, "I'm Carla DuPree. I bought the house on the cliff and I need furniture that will match the house." She paused and then quickly added, "A bed and a table. There is no furniture in the house and since I plan on staying there during remodeling, I will need a place to sleep and eat."

The salesman blushed. He had heard the cliff house had been sold, but he didn't know Carla. "I'm sorry," he quickly mumbled, hanging his head. "You're too pretty to be buying furniture by yourself." He paused, hoping he had not made matters worse by his last comment. "Well, as you can see, we carry the new Danish

modern style that has simple straight lines and sets low to the floor."
He looked around carefully and lowered his voice, "I think the cliff
house screams for Victorian furniture. Now don't tell anyone I said
that." He looked all around again.

"I do too," Carla said with some relief in her voice. "Do you
know where I can find that or at least a similar style?" The salesman
motioned for her to head to the door.

"There are several antique stores nearby on the Pacific Coast
Highway and an old furniture store two towns north of here. The
folks moving here are mostly young professionals and they want all
new styles. I think you have more class than them."

"More good news." Carla thought to herself, "Young professionals are always trying to impress people. They take their friends
and clients to expensive places and pay too much. They will like
my place."

Carla smiled sheepishly and then thanked the salesman profusely. "I hope you'll come to my restaurant when it opens."

They shook hands and Carla headed to the hardware store. She
was right. They had business cards for several carpenters and cleaning services. Carla noticed a star drawn in one corner of one of the
cards. She looked up at the store manager. He winked. She got the
message. He was a businessman and couldn't recommend one company over another, but he felt Carla was vulnerable and wanted to
protect her. Carla paid for her purchase of three scrub buckets, two
boxes of Spic-and-Span, two mops, and a package of cleaning cloths.
It was one o'clock now and she wanted Wanda's advice.

CHAPTER ELEVEN

Wanda

Wanda grew up in Otra Vez and knew all the businesses and pretty much every person in town. She was still friends with her high-school classmates but didn't see much of them anymore. They were married with children and she wasn't. In a 1950s small town, a girl over thirty was considered a spinster, and was expected to remain that way for the rest of her life.

Wanda didn't feel like a spinster. She enjoyed her work at the diner. The morning rush was mostly locals who kept her up to date on local happenings. The lunch crunch was mostly tourists. Wanda especially liked this group. She would watch the license plates to see where folks were from. Places she didn't expect to ever see. She would ask and the diners would happily tell her where they were from and where they were headed. This group had the best tippers. Sometimes they would leave a postcard from where they had been for her along with the tip. She had quite a collection she kept behind the counter. The evening customers were sparse. Usually just people in a hurry to get somewhere else.

It was the end of the morning rush the first time Carla had stopped at the diner. When Wanda saw Carla's New York license plate, she took an immediate interest in her. Carla did not react the same way until after she saw the house on top of the cliff. She wanted information and the only person who had spoken to her was Wanda. Being desperate, she had headed to the diner hoping Wanda might be there. Of course Wanda was and had welcomed Carla. The way Wanda welcomed her and readily answered her questions put Carla at ease. Their friendship blossomed from there and continued to grow each time Carla had a meal there.

By the time Carla had finished with the furniture salesman and the hardware manager, it was the end of the lunch crunch at the diner. Wanda smiled when she saw Carla enter. Carla ordered a bowl of chicken-noodle soup with a slice of thick crusty bread from the Bagonski Culinary School. "How's things shaking?" Wanda asked Carla when she brought her coffee.

"Good, I think," Carla said a bit nervously. She showed Wanda the business cards she had gotten at the hardware store. Wanda told Carla what she knew and what she had heard about the different contractors. Often the two were not the same.

"I still need a bed and table," Carla lamented. "The salesman at the furniture store suggested I try some antique stores."

At the mention of antique stores, Wanda became very excited. "I want to go with you," she nearly shouted. "I love antiquing." This was good news for Carla. Antiquing was completely new to her, and the thought of bargaining made her cringe.

"When can you go?" Carla asked.

"Well, not till three today. And that's not good for antiquing. By that time, they are all haggled out. How about we leave at nine tomorrow? I'll take the day off and we can make it a day."

Carla hesitated. Spending an entire day shopping was not her idea of a good time. But she sure could use Wanda's help. "Let's do it!" she exclaimed. Carla paid for her soup and drove her car back to the town square. She didn't know why, but she had a tickling desire to tell the old man on the bench that the cliff house was now hers.

She walked purposely directly to the old man and sat on the bench. He didn't move or acknowledge her. "I own the cliff house," she said.

"I know," he said still not looking at her.

Carla sighed. "I have the name of a carpenter and a cleaning service. I need a landscaper," she said trying to get him to talk.

"Go to Garcia's Gardens. Tell them I sent you."

"I don't know your name," Carla said with anticipation, expecting him to tell her. The old man lowered his newspaper and looked at her. His mouth was pulled up on the right side and his right eye was pulled down. She felt his disapproval piercing her very heart. How could she have spoken to him so often and not bothered to learn his name? Her face reddened. He snapped his paper back into position and resumed his reading. Carla rose and walked back to her car. Her shoulders were not as straight as when she came. The old man lowered his paper an inch and watched her walk away. A slight smile touched his lips.

At Garcia's Gardens, Carla was checking out the rose bushes when Jose approached her. "May I help you, ma'am?"

"I recently bought the cliff house and I need a landscaper. The old man on the bench in the town square told me to come here. He said to tell you he sent me."

Jose's face went blank. He turned to John who was watering the roses. John, bending over slightly to keep from laughing, almost squirted both Carla and Jose. "I suppose he said you would get a discount for mentioning him," Jose said suspiciously.

"Well, no. No he didn't. But that would be nice."

Jose looked at John. John turned his back toward them. "We do the best work. We can help you. We can be there tomorrow morning."

"Oh, I can't make tomorrow morning. I have other plans. How about the next day?"

"We will inspect the grounds tomorrow and bring you a pre-liminary plan the next day if that is okay with you."

Carla was stunned at the response. She wasn't used to services being offered so quickly. He hadn't even checked her out. She glanced around. There were lots of flowers and shrubs and they all looked healthy and well cared for. This was not an unimportant operation. "I will need a new fence along the cliff. Can you take care of that?"

"We can take care of all your landscaping needs, ma'am. We will do a good job and you will not need to worry about a thing."

"Thank you," Carla replied warily as she reached out her hand to shake Jose's. Jose wiped his hand on his jeans before shaking Carla's.

Carla wasn't sure about this transaction. For some reason she was just not at ease. Maybe it was her New York skepticism. She needed to learn more about the old man. "Tomorrow. Tomorrow on the way to the antique stores I will ask Wanda," she decided.

CHAPTER TWELVE

Antiquing

At nine in the morning, Wanda, dressed in jeans with the cuffs rolled up and a plaid shirt, was chomping at the bit. "Hurry, Carla. We want to get there early, before the haggling has worn everyone out." Carla, dressed in slacks and a silk shirt, was not as enthusiastic. She had no experience with haggling or antiques. She would be completely dependent on Wanda, and she had no knowledge of Wanda's expertise. Looking at Wanda's well-used 1941 Ford Coupe, Carla offered, "I can drive my car."

"No way! If they see a new car, the price goes up," Wanda warned.

Being nervous brought back unpleasant memories to Carla. "This is my new life," she reminded herself. "I am going to try new things. If I don't like it, I can say no. I can just say no." She repeated "just say no" a few more times so it would stick in her brain. She would not be easily led this time. She was smarter now. She learned how to follow her gut, and she was going to do that. "Just say no," she repeated again.

"Isn't this fun?" Wanda giggled. "I haven't been on a girl's day in a very long time. This is going to be so much fun."

Wanda was so excited, Carla had to smile. "Me, too." Carla took a deep breath. "Wanda, do you know the old man that sets on the bench in the town square?"

"Sure. Everyone does. He's a great old man. He owns Garcia's Gardens. You should go there for landscaping advice. He learned the business at an agricultural school in southern California. And he has sent all his employees there for training at his expense."

"So that's it," Carla thought cynically, "He's planning on making a mint off me."

Wanda continued, "The first antique store is about one mile ahead. If we are successful there, we can go to the café right next to it. The café has a lot of local flavor. If not, there are a few more off the mountain road."

"I'd like to know more about the old man," Carla said.

"Why? Because if you are planning on taking advantage of him, I will not help you."

"Oh, no. It's just that he has been very nice to me and I don't understand it."

Wanda laughed. "You're not in New York anymore, Carla."

Carla gave a short chuckle. "That's for sure. Is that the antique store up there on the right?"

"That's the first."

"The first! How many are there?"

"Well, I only know about five. If there are any new ones, they usually tell me about them and give me the scoop on them. You know. Is their stuff any good, is it real, is it over-priced? The ones I go to are all reputable. They just haggle for the fun of it."

Carla was beginning to feel panicky. All she wanted was a bed and table. How could buying that be so involved? Wanda pulled into the first antique store parking lot. "Here we are!" she shouted and jumped out of the car. She was halfway to the store before Carla opened her door.

Once out of the car, Carla looked all around. It wasn't New York's Herald's Square, but it was clean and neat. At Wanda's urging, she hurried over to the entrance. Wanda's eyes glowed as she looked over the vast array of old stuff. Carla checked out her escape route. "I can always just say no," kept running through her mind.

"Here, here, Carla. Look at these beautiful dishes."

"I'm looking for a bed and table. Not dishes," Carla reminded Wanda.

"It doesn't hurt to look," Wanda replied, "Besides, if you don't look, you might miss something you really want."

Carla didn't reply. She followed Wanda on through the store to the furniture section. There were a few beds and several tables. The tables impressed Carla, but the beds weren't exactly right. She walked over to one gate-leg table, and while she was scrutinizing it, the salesman walked over. "That is a particularly fine piece. You won't find another like it. And the price is more than fair."

"It's $75 and has scratches," Wanda took over.

"Some furniture polish and those scratches will never show again."

"Does it wobble?"

"Not that I know of." The salesman's eyes were shining. He was ready for the show.

Wanda turned to Carla, "Are you interested?" Carla nodded yes. Turning to the salesman, Wanda shifted to her right foot and tilted her head. "Are you going to open it?" The salesman quickly moved a chair and another table out of the way and began opening the table. Wanda grabbed the closest leaf and began raising it.

The salesman grabbed the other side of the same leaf. "Let me help." The table opened from two feet to ten feet with three leaves. It was sturdy and there were no deep scratches. It would suit multiple needs for Carla.

Carla was opening her mouth to say she would take it when Wanda said, "$50 and not a penny more. It's not mahogany so that's all it's worth." Carla looked at her in disbelief.

The salesman smiled. "Aww. So we have here a lady who knows her antiques."

Wanda tilted her head to the side. "That we do."

"In that case, since you are obviously an appreciator of fine furniture, I'll sell it to you for $65."

Carla extended her hand to close the deal, but Wanda stood firm. "That does include delivery?" she half questioned and half ordered.

The salesman grinned. "You drive a hard bargain. Is there anything else I can help you with? We have some lovely dining chairs." Carla's eyes opened wide. She was going to need some of those.

"Another time," Wanda smiled, shook the salesman's hand, and poked Carla in the side. Carla said nothing. The salesman wrote up the sale. Carla paid, and they headed to the front door a different way than they entered.

Carla stopped short. Hanging on the wall in front of them was a four-by-five-foot painting of a beautiful woman dressed in red. The salesman caught her look. "That's the Prospector's lady."

Carla spun around. "It has to be the Prospector who built my house. Wanda, it's the perfect fit for the large blank wall by the stairs," she gushed.

"Another time," Wanda said as she pushed Carla out the door. "Carla, you never let them know when you want something. The price goes up."

"Otra Vez, another time." Carla mumbled. "Wanda, that painting needs to come home to the cliff house."

"Carla. You gave the salesman your address. He knows you live at the cliff house. He was working you."

"Wanda, I saw the name on the bottom of the painting. It said 'The Prospector's Lady.'"

Wanda looked directly into Carla's eyes. "That's spooky. Come on. We're going to the next shop to get you a bed."

Carla found a full-size, four-poster bed at the next shop. This time she let Wanda haggle with no interference.

They had lunch in a local café attached to an ESSO gas station, then headed home. Wanda was ecstatic. Carla was very happy. She watched the route they took closely. She fully intended to return and get "The Prospector's Lady." The cliff house was hers first. She belongs there and Carla didn't care how much she cost.

CHAPTER THIRTEEN

The Painting

As promised, the telephone company arrived bright and early the next morning. While they were connecting the telephone lines, the landscaper, Juan Reyes from Garcia's Gardens, came with a full set of plans for the property. Carla wanted them all to leave so she could hurry back to the antique shop and buy "The Prospector's Lady" portrait before someone else did.

The telephone people worked quickly connecting both lines to the main phone in the hallway near the bottom of the second-floor stairs. Extensions for both lines were installed in the kitchen; in the room beside the kitchen, which was to be Carla's office; and in the room directly above the kitchen, which was Carla's private room. "That's the most extensions we've ever installed in one house," the installation supervisor said.

"I'm opening a restaurant," Carla smiled and added. "I hope you will come for dinner."

The supervisor looked around. "It's going to be beautiful. Probably expensive, too."

"Well, yes. But I hope you come anyway," Carla laughed as she signed the receipt.

The supervisor thanked her, wished her good luck with her restaurant, and left.

Carla took a deep breath. It was now ten o'clock. She wanted to leave, but the landscaper was still there. He had walked along the cliff and made a few more notes. Carla went to greet him and to try to hurry him along. His plans were very detailed. Much more detailed than Carla wanted to take time to review. She noted that the fence running along the cliff and back to each side of the house was four feet high. "Four feet sounds high for the fence. I think three feet would be better."

"Miss DuPree, many men are six feet tall. A three-foot fence is only half as high as them. If they lean too far, they may topple clear over the cliff." Carla looked at him skeptically and wondered if he was making fun of her. As she thought about the situation, she could see he was right. Under some circumstances, a lot of people's common sense and balance are compromised.

"Miss DuPree, as the plans show, the top posts of the fence are four feet and stand eighteen inches apart. Shorter, three-foot posts are between the tall posts. That way, the view is not blocked, but access to the cliff is. It is a very pretty design with curls and rosettes. We considered putting arrow heads on top of the tall posts, but decided it would give a threatening feeling, and you are much too sweet to be threatening."

Carla could feel herself softening. She had to remind herself not to be taken in by compliments. Looking back at the plans, she asked, "Exactly where are these flower gardens going to be?"

Juan led her along where a path would follow the curve of the cliff. He pointed out the garden areas as they walked and explained which flowers would be where. Carla knew tulips and roses. The flowers he named (bougainvillea, wisteria, jasmine) sounded beautiful, but she didn't know any of them. Hoping he wouldn't notice, she just listened. "They are the experts. Plants can always be changed. I'll take their advice for now," she decided.

Juan explained where the parking lot would be and how they planned to camouflage the view of it. He mentioned the redwood trees and suggested they could be used to attract customers. Carla's mind had turned to mush. She wanted to go get "The Prospector's Lady," and all other talk just swirled around in her head making her anxious. "The plans sound wonderful, Juan. Can you leave them with me so I can give them a second look?"

"Of course. And if you have any questions, please call me. My number is on the cover sheet and I see you now have a telephone."

Carla smiled. "I see what makes you so good. You don't miss a thing."

Juan smiled and shook Carla's hand. "Till you call," he said and left.

Carla ran inside, grabbed her purse, and hurried to her car. It was almost noon. Wanda said the salesmen were all haggled out after lunch and she couldn't get a good price. "I don't care about a good price. I want that picture," Carla shouted out loud and stepped on the gas.

It was a short drive to the antique store and no cars were in the parking lot. Carla hurried out of her car and rushed into the store directly to "The Prospector's Lady." It was still there. She thought, "Well, I already broke two of Wanda's rules. It's lunch time and I practically told them outright I want that picture. I might as well go ahead and pay full price." Looking around she noticed she was the only customer in the store and she didn't see yesterday's salesman. Looking back at the painting, she did her best not to drool. She ran her finger over the gold frame. Roses were carved along all the edges. Love birds were carved at the top corners. A carved ribbon curved gracefully across the bottom.

An elderly man with wrinkled, leathery skin approached her. He was hunched over and walked very slowly, but his smile would win every heart.

"Well hello, lass. She's a beautiful lady isn't she? She was the Prospector's lady," the elderly man said.

A smile covered Carla's face before she could stop it. "I read that. It's on the bottom of the frame. I will offer you $75 for it." Then, remembering Wanda's advice, she added, "That's including delivery."

The elderly man reached out his hand. "I'm Shamus O'Leary. Folks call me Sam. Do you know who the Prospector was?"

"No. Well, sort of," Carla answered hesitantly as she shook his hand.

Sam continued, "The Prospector struck gold in Colorado, married this beautiful dance hall girl, and brought her here to California. He built a mansion for her on the cliff overlooking Otra Vez. But life there was too quiet for her. She found the ocean waves monotonous and the town boring. Otra Vez was much smaller then.

The cove hadn't been filled in yet. I was told the Prospector and the lady moved to Nevada, where he built her a saloon."

"So you are saying the ghost is not the Prospector's lady," Carla teased.

"No. No. She would be the Sea Captain's wife."

At that moment yesterday's salesman walked in. He recognized Carla immediately. Sam smiled. "This is my grandson. We call him Sammy after me," he beamed as he told Carla.

Sammy had seen the 1950 Ford with New York license plates and suspected it was Carla's. "Grandpa, did this woman tell you she wants 'The Prospector's Lady' and that the cliff house is hers?"

"Aye, she offered us $75."

"And that includes delivery," Carla added.

"The price is $100, and well worth it. It is an original oil painting dated 1855." Sammy figured anyone with a new car could pay full price.

"'That's almost a hundred years," Carla gushed. "And it's part of the history of the area. And you're only charging less than $1 a year!"

Sammy was bemused. "You don't know much about haggling do you?"

Carla blushed, "No."

"Well, since I haven't delivered your table yet, I will throw in the delivery."

Carla threw her hands in the air and shouted, "Sold!"

Sam was floored. What just happened? He was going to sell her the painting for $75 including delivery, and now she was happily paying $100. A look of confusion covered his face. Carla put her hand on his arm. "The history lesson made the picture worth every penny of $100. I would very much like to hear about the Sea Captain. And more about the cove, how it grew. May I come back another time for another story?"

"And to buy something," Sammy interjected.

"Aye, but don't wait too long. I'm pretty old," Sam said.

Carla laughed and added, "I hope you will come to my restaurant sometime."

She paid for the picture, including the story, and headed to Otra Vez. She couldn't wait to tell Wanda about her first "successful" haggle.

CHAPTER FOURTEEN

Renovations Begin

Carla did a little skip into the Seaside Diner. "Well, aren't you the happy one," Wanda teased. "What happened?"

"Wanda, it was wonderful, exhilarating, energizing, satisfying and any other word you can think of. I did it. I did it all by myself."

"Did what?"

"I haggled for 'The Prospector's Lady' portrait and I got it."

"How much did you pay?"

"$100."

"That's full price!" Wanda exclaimed, almost dropping the dirty dishes she was carrying.

"Yes, but I got the story with it." There was no squelching Carla's joy.

"When will they deliver it? You aren't paying for delivery are you?" Wanda sounded accusatory.

"No. I did just what you did. I said delivery included and they agreed."

Wanda sighed. At least she learned that.

"Anyway, they are to deliver it with the table tomorrow. By the way, I now have a phone. And Juan from Garcia's Gardens brought by his landscaping plans. I need to review them tonight. The remodeling contractor is scheduled for tomorrow. It's happening Wanda. My dream is happening." Carla gave a little clap.

Wanda smiled. It was good to see her friend so happy. "I knew it would. I can come over late tomorrow afternoon to give advice if you want."

"That would be great. Can I have a coffee and a Bagonski Danish to go? I have to get to the utility office before they close or my electric might be turned off." Wanda handed Carla a bagged coffee and Danish. "See you tomorrow," Carla called as she jogged to her car. She was still excited.

The utility office was not busy. The clerk recognized Carla, grabbed some papers, and came right over. "How are you today, Miss DuPree?" Carla still marveled at the friendliness of the people in this town.

"I'm fine. I brought the papers you said I would need." She handed the papers to the clerk.

The clerk looked them over, then went to the back room and opened a very large ledger book. After a few minutes, she returned with a smile on her face. "Everything is in order. Please sign here. We will transfer all the billing records to your name. We are very happy you have chosen our wonderful little town to build your retreat."

Carla smiled. How fast word travels here. She couldn't remember who she told about plans for a retreat, but it wasn't everyone. "Thank you. I'm glad I'm here too."

It was only the middle of the afternoon when Carla was leaving the utility office. The sky was clear and the air was sweet. "This is a good time to tour the town. I really need to know more about it," she reasoned. Most if not all of the businesses were located in the center part of the cove around the town square. "This must be the part they filled," Carla noted. She drove on past the town square on the main boulevard running through the town. The ocean side of the cove was the well-kept sandy beach. Nothing blocked the view of the calm Pacific Ocean.

Mountains on the north and south sides of the cove had streets lined with houses. The east side was her cliff. A single street with houses stretched across the bottom of the cliff. The houses on the lower streets were modest, mostly bungalows with tiny yards. Higher up were more bungalows and a few two-story colonials. Carla recognized the one Sue tried to sell her. There were two one-story modern houses with car patios that looked very out of place in this quaint seaside town.

About three-quarters of the way up on the north mountain was a two-story red brick federal-style house. Palm trees waved behind a red-brick wall surrounding the house. She supposed gardens were hidden behind the wall. "There's money there." Carla's experience had taught her how to recognize money.

Across from the federal-style house, three-quarters of the way up on the south mountain, was a two-story white stucco house with a white stucco wall around it. Carla looked back and forth between the two houses. "There's a story here. Maybe Wanda knows it. If not, maybe Sam does. I'll find it. I have to. Something like this usually has something to do with a feud, and I can't afford to take sides in a feud. One can never tell when something like that will explode."

Making a mental note of what she had seen, she turned her car and headed back to the town square. She had shopped in some of the stores, but wanted a better look. Often things are missed when concentrating on shopping. She parked her car at the corner closest to the beach and began her tour. She passed a gift shop, the Clips & Curls shop, and the furniture store and was in front of the jewelry store when she saw the black limousine. It was on the far side of the square moving slowly in her direction. She turned her back to the street, pretending she was looking at the jewelry in the window. In truth, every muscle in her body was stiff, her breathing tight.

It felt like it was that day in New York all over again. She and her boss, Winston, were walking to lunch. They were almost at the restaurant when he pushed her into a jewelry store. "Pick out a bracelet," he snapped at her. Carla liked jewelry and proceeded to do as ordered. Winston stood behind a display case where he could keep his eye on the street, but not be seen, while she chose the diamond-studded ankle bracelet. Turning to show it to Winston, she saw the limousine moving slowly down the street. Then she heard the shot. Winston told the clerk to put the bracelet on his tab, told Carla he had to get back to work, and hurried out the door, leaving her alone. She now realized she should have left then. Carla shivered, trying to shake off the memory.

Being cautious, she waited till the limousine completed its journey around the square and headed out of town. Just like on her first day, no one else seemed to notice. She moved swiftly back to her car, retrieved her coffee and Danish, and walked to the beach.

The coffee was cold, and the air was warm. A good combination. The cheese Danish was better than she expected, and relaxing for fifteen minutes calmed her down. When the sun was forty-five degrees above the horizon, Carla took her shoes off and headed to the ocean. The waves were calm. She tipped one foot in to test the temperature. "Awwwwww." It felt good. She moved her other foot into the water and enjoyed the waves washing over her toes.

Phillip Bagonski happened to be driving past the beach and saw Carla standing on the ocean edge. Pulling into a parking space (there are always parking spaces available in Otra Vez), he checked to see if she was alone. Noting she was, he slipped his car into park. As he scanned the beach to see who else might be there, he made his way to Carla. She didn't see him coming and when he spoke, she nearly lost her balance. "I didn't mean to scare you."

"You didn't. Just surprised me. I'm a bit nervous."

"Why?"

"What do you know about that limousine that was circling the square?"

"Not much. Why? Do you want to ride in a limo?" Phillip teased.

Phillip's answer did not put Carla at ease. Not knowing the story of the limo, she decided it wisest not to pursue it any further. "What are you doing here?" she asked.

"I saw you. How are things going? Are you ready for my help?" Phillip said smoothly—so smoothly that Carla forgot she was standing on sand in the ocean. A wave, small though it was, washed the sand from under her feet.

"Aaaaaaaah!" she yelled as she flailed her arms, hitting Phillip on the side of his head and falling against his chest. Phillip reacted quickly, wrapping his arms around her. Embarrassed, she mumbled, "Thanks," and stepped toward land.

"Don't let that throw you," he laughed. "Here, I'll take my shoes off and we can both walk along the shore and hold each other up." Carla stood on the beach while Phillip took his shoes off and they walked south along the shoreline. They talked about the weather, the fish they could see jumping in the ocean, and the ship that was barely on this side of the horizon. Safe topics.

They turned and the red brick house three-quarters up the mountain on the north side of town caught Carla's eye. "See that red house up there? Do you know whose it is?"

A quizzical look passed over Phillip's face, then turned into a half grin. His eyes skimmed over Carla from the top of her head to her toes, settling on her eyes. She wasn't the first girl who caught Phillip's eye. But she was different from the others. She was intelligent, independent, and had that East Coast sophistication. He wanted to sweep her up and carry her to the red brick house. Instead he warned himself he might scare her off. "It's mine. Do you want to go see it?"

Carla blushed. What was he asking? Did she want to see it? Of course. Otherwise she wouldn't have mentioned it. But what did he mean, "see it"? See what? Was this him insinuating or her imagining what might happen? He was holding her hand and it felt good. He was tall, good-looking, blond with a California tan, muscular, and kind. She was facing going back to a big empty house by herself. "I didn't know. Honest, I didn't know. I think I better take a raincheck on that," she stammered.

Phillip chuckled. "I'm going to hold you to that," he said with a crooked little smile. They walked back to their cars. Remembering the office girls' advice to strike while the iron's hot, Phillip asked, "Can I collect on my raincheck?"

Every fiber of her being wanted to say yes. But that nasty old common sense reared its head. Carla looked down and softly said, "I have a busy day tomorrow."

Phillip reached out and took her hands in his, pulling her close. He kissed her on her forehead, smiled, and said, "Till next time."

The kiss about did her in. "Till next time," Carla repeated weakly and pulled her hands away before she made a fool of herself. Turning quickly, she walked slowly back to her car, hoping he might come after her but knowing it was too soon. She didn't know anything about him. Besides, tomorrow was going to be a busy day.

CHAPTER FIFTEEN

Phillip

Phillip watched Carla drive away. What had he done? He was always cautious. Never did anything irrational. No spur of the moment actions. Always checked things out before proceeding with anything, even double-checking which flour to use in cake recipes.

Now, just a few days ago, he gave information about the cliff house to this girl he didn't know. Wasn't even sure what she would do with it or to whom she might pass it on. Didn't even know where she came from. Except her license plate said New York, and New York is a big state. He had no idea of her background. No one seemed to know how or why she came to Otra Vez. It seemed no one cared. Maybe he should ask the sheriff to check her out. And why? Why did he pull her against him and kiss her?

What must she think of him now? She wasn't like any of the many other girls he had dated. She had brains and ambition. Was she using him? How would he know? She had offered to pay for his help. That didn't sound like she was taking advantage of him. Still, would she pay what he was worth or would she try to use her other attributes to keep hold of her cash?

True, she was pretty. But he had dated lots of pretty girls. He never had trouble getting a date when he wanted one. And sometimes when he didn't. Carla had pulled away from him. She was the one who stopped the evening. He wasn't used to that. He usually had trouble ending the evening. "After all," he admitted, "I am quite a catch."

He saw the lights come on at the cliff house. Carla was home. "Play it cool," he told himself, "don't push her. Once she knows what a great guy I am, she will beg me to kiss her." He laughed. "Who am I kidding? A girl like Carla can have anyone she wants. I hope it's me."

Carla walked to the edge of the cliff overlooking Phillip's house. It was dark, no lights were shining. She figured he must have gone back to the beach. "Next time," she thought, "if there is a next time, I will not be in such a hurry to leave."

CHAPTER SIXTEEN

It Is Happening

Carla sat on the front porch watching the waves roll in as she drank her morning coffee. Things were beginning to happen very fast. "Too fast," she worried. "Maybe I should slow things down a bit. But time is money and this is costing me plenty as it is." Her thoughts were interrupted by a middle-aged man, dressed in a rumpled summer suit, slowly walking across the front yard as he studied the house.

"Good day, Ma'am. I hope I didn't startle you. I'm Walter Ivenson from Pacific Coast Architects. A Mr. Ron Gunderson from New York called us and asked us to evaluate this property."

Carla smothered a chuckle. It was just like Ron to do that. "I know Mr. Gunderson. He is trying to protect my money," she smiled. "And he is right. I don't know much about building structures. I have the name of a carpenter, but could use some advice on major repairs."

"Who is the carpenter?"

Carla went inside and got the business card with the hand-written star in the corner. "It's Gustav Heinz," she said as she handed the card to Walter.

"I know him. We have used him on a number of our remodel jobs. He's easy to work with and extremely honest. Have you called him yet?"

"No. That's on my to-do list for today."

Walter cupped his chin in his right hand and stared at his papers. "Let me call him. I'll see if he can meet me here and we can make our evaluations and suggestions together. After all, as they say, two heads are better than one."

"Only if one is not a cabbage," Carla replied. It took a minute for Walter to understand. Then he howled thunderously. "You may use my phone if you like," Carla offered.

While Walter was calling Gustav, Carla looked over the landscaping plans Juan from Garcia's Gardens left. She felt overwhelmed. "You don't know anything about flowers," she told herself. "You don't even know what these flowers look like." It was true. She knew it was true. "Best I take their advice," she acknowledged and breathed a sigh of relief. "I'll call them as soon as Walter leaves."

Walter came back to the porch just as Carla was folding the landscaping plans. "Those the landscaping plans?" he asked.

Carla nodded. "I'm afraid I don't understand them as well as I should. Truth be told, tulips and roses are the only flowers I know."

"Those plans are from Garcia's Gardens," Walter more stated than asked. Carla nodded again. "Then you don't need to worry. They are the best."

"Do you know Mr. Garcia?"

"Everyone knows Mr. Garcia. That statue in the park should be him instead of that S.O.B., Mr. Richardson."

"Why?"

"Mr. Garcia is a kind, humble man who helps anyone. It doesn't matter if they are rich or poor, smart or dumb, arrogant or not. And Mr. Richardson almost broke Mr. Garcia's back." Walter shook his head, as if trying to clear the thought, and changed the subject. "I spoke with Gustav. He is going to meet me here at one o'clock, if that is OK with you."

The furrows on Walter's head had deepened. It seemed the discussion about Mr. Garcia had upset him. Carla wanted to know more, but thought it better not to ask right now. "That's fine with me."

Walter bowed his head slightly, turned, and walked back to his truck.

It was ten in the morning. Carla went inside and called Garcia's Gardens. Juan answered the phone and was very pleased when she said the plans were fine. "I'll be up later today to take some more measurements and get started. Thank you for trusting us with your beautiful property."

At 12:30, Carla heard a rumbling noise coming from the trees in the back of the house. It was Sammy delivering her table and "The Prospector's Lady" portrait. His grandfather, Sam, was with him. Carla ran out to meet them.

"I hope you don't mind my grandfather coming along. He hasn't been here in almost a decade and wanted to see how things have changed."

"Of course not. Welcome, Sam. Maybe we'll have some time for a history lesson."

"We're here to work. Not give out more free stuff," Sammy objected. "I'm going to need some help unloading this stuff."

"I'm the only one here. So I guess I'm your help," Carla snapped back.

"I can help," Sam declared. "Aye, I'm well on my way over the hill, but I'm still breathing."

Right then, Walter from Pacific Coast Architects arrived, with Gustav right behind him. Gustav was a tall, broad-shouldered man with muscles bulging from his shirt sleeves. As soon as he saw Sammy, he headed straight to him. The two men slapped each other on the back and began catching up. Apparently, they knew each other ever since their teen antics. "Grandpa," Sammy said, "why don't you go see the ocean? Gustav and I will get this stuff inside."

"I'll show you where I want the portrait hung," Carla said and headed to the house.

"Miss DuPree," Walter stopped her, "you can't hang that picture until we evaluate the house and make sure the wall is sturdy enough to hold it. You don't want it to fall and break, or worse, land on someone." Carla stopped in her tracks. She had never considered the plaster on the walls might be crumbly.

"Of course. After you," she said and stepped out of the way.

"Don't you worry, lass," Sam said softly, "These boys can fix anything that's broken and they know what's not. Come walk with me to the front porch."

Carla took him by his elbow and they walked around the south side of the house. "Well faith and begorra!" Sam said when the ocean came in view. "It is just as I remember."

Carla chuckled and helped him up the porch steps for a better view. "Please, lass, let me tell you the story of the Captain's wife. Tis a sad tale for sure. But one you should know, now that this house is yours. I mean, if you are going to be visited by ghosts, at least you should know why."

Carla wanted to say she didn't believe in ghosts, but Sam was so sincere, she decided to be quiet.

"The Captain and his wife had a son. A good boy, blond with rosy cheeks, and long legs. When he was old enough, the Captain would take the boy on short voyages. The boy loved the ocean. The travels and ocean were good for him, and he grew strong and healthy." Sam paused. "But the missus was not so strong. Folks said she didn't eat or sleep when the Captain was at sea. They said all she did was pace across the cliff." Sam waved his arm for emphasis. "There was an epidemic came through here, some kind of flu. And the wife caught it. The Captain was home and he stayed by her side day and night. The doctor came by daily to check on her. The Captain hired nurses to care for her. Sadly it was all to no avail. She died. The Captain buried her back among the trees. He was distraught. He couldn't stand her being in the ground. So he took the boy and they sailed away. He never came back. The missus walks the cliff every night looking for him. Aye, lass, it is a true story, sad to tell."

Carla didn't know what to say. "He never came back?"

"Never," Sam repeated. Carla stared at the cliff. What else could she do? For sure it was a sad story. Maybe the Chinese characters on the red room's walls were not happy sayings. Maybe they were mourning chants. She couldn't or wouldn't live in a house with sad mourning chants written on the walls. She had to find someone who could interpret them.

"OK, Grandpa, it's time to go," Sammy burst through the front door, breaking the silence.

"I've enjoyed talking with you, lass," Sam said as he struggled to his feet.

"The pleasure is all mine," Carla said graciously. "I do hope you will come back when my restaurant is open and we can talk some more." Sam smiled, turned, and hobbled off the porch with Sammy's help.

As promised, Juan from Garcia's Gardens arrived with several helpers. The helpers began tearing down the rusty old wrought-iron fence along the cliff edge. Juan came directly to Carla with some papers to sign. As she was signing the papers, Walter and Gustav came out of the house. It was like a homecoming. Walter, Gustav, and Juan all knew each other. Carla was beginning to wonder if this was small town or if they were in cahoots, all getting ready to take advantage of her. They wouldn't be the first. "Not this time," Carla vowed to herself. She was smarter, more experienced now and she was not going to be exploited or manipulated by anyone.

Her wondering was cut short when Wanda arrived. Gustav stood straighter, which didn't seem possible a minute ago, his eyes opened wide and his cheeks reddened. "Go for it Gustav," Juan said.

"Go on," Walter encouraged. Gustav took three steps toward Wanda.

Wanda's face turned pink. She reached up and smoothed her hair. She caught her green cardigan sweater in the car door when she shut it. Juan elbowed Gustav, "Help her, you big lug."

Gustav hurried to Wanda and opened the car door for her. Wanda freed her sweater from the door's grasp and looked at the ground. She tried to walk, but her feet just shuffled. Finally, she managed to say, "Thank you."

Gustav shrugged his shoulders, "It was nothing." Walter and Juan gave him a thumbs-up. Carla wasn't sure what she had just seen.

"Why don't we all have a cup of coffee while we discuss what needs to be done?" It was the best suggestion Carla could come up with.

The table was placed straight in from the front door, centered below the large window and second-floor walkway. Wanda helped Carla serve the coffee by giving Gustav the biggest mug. She had fixed it exactly the way he liked it: half milk and two spoons of sugar. All the others helped themselves. Walter was the first to speak.

"Miss DuPree."

"Please call me Carla."

"Sure. You're one of us now, so that will be acceptable," Walter responded. "And you should call me Walt." Carla hoped that meant they would not take advantage of her. Walt continued, "We have inspected the roof, basement, structure, and walls of this house and find it generally in good shape. We did not see any major repairs needed. However, we would like to check the large window on the second-floor walkway a little further. It appears to have been added after the house was completed. Are there any changes you had in mind?"

"Please do a thorough check on that window. I want customers to see that view from the front door as soon as they enter, and from the registration desk, which I want right here where we are sitting."

"That's a very good idea," Juan said. "The window makes a nice frame around the redwood trees at the back of the property." Everyone turned their heads and looked. There was no need to stand to see the redwoods. "Mr. Garcia told me the naturalist, I can't remember his name, that lived here called it 'heart and soul,' heart for the ocean and soul for the redwoods."

"I heard the same thing. I can't remember his name either. I was told he is the one who contacted the National Forest Service about protection for those three redwoods. Made the whole community angry. No one wants their land use limited," Walt added authoritatively.

"He didn't do it alone," Juan interjected. "Town gossip has it he knew John Muir and Audubon. They say Ralph Waldo Emerson helped him get the designation." Carla's head was beginning to spin with all this historical information. She needed to get it written down so she could follow up on it later. Perhaps she could use this for some sort of publicity.

"Is there anything else you want?" Walt asked Carla.

"I want 'The Prospector's Lady' portrait hung on that wall." She motioned to the wall by the stairs leading up to the walkway. The three men frowned.

"That wall is twenty feet high and nineteen feet wide. Your picture will get lost on that wall," Walt said softly. Juan nodded his head in agreement.

Wanda looked at Gustav. Gustav lowered his head and turned it slowly side to side. Wanda pulled her eyes down, wrinkling her nose. She moved her mouth to one side, took a deep breath, and threw an encouraging look at Gustav. Gustav said nothing. "Gustav's sister is an interior designer. And she's really good." Pausing, Wanda threw another look at Gustav. He tightened his lips into a straight short smile of approval.

"That's a great idea," Juan agreed. "I've seen her work. She could help you spruce up all the rooms. No pun intended," he added sheepishly. Muffled laughs and groans sounded around the table.

"Gustav," Carla said softly, "Please have your sister call me."

"Yes Ma'am. Her name is Gertrude," Gustav looked at Wanda. Wanda gave him a smug smile that said, "See, I'm right."

"Phillip will be here tomorrow afternoon to do a final check of the kitchen. Walt, can you be here also?" Carla asked.

"Be happy to."

"Gustav, when do you think you will be starting?'

Gustav checked his notes. "I believe the south addition with the parquet floor only needs cleaning. I will get that started tomorrow. I suggest only repairing the wallpaper in the two original front rooms. If you like the Chinese characters in the north addition, I will get someone I know to repair the worn away lettering. I think the hallways only need some minor plaster repairs and painting. I will bring some samples with me tomorrow if you agree."

"I would like to know the meaning of the Chinese characters before it is repaired. I only want happy thoughts in this marvelous house."

"Of course," Gustav agreed, adding a note on his list of items.

"Tomorrow will be a fine time to start," Carla said, making a note on the paper in front of her. "Oh, one more thing, Juan, Sam told me the Captain's wife is buried somewhere on the property. I would like to preserve it some way."

"We'll look for it, Ma'am. You know it was a long time ago. It would be overgrown by now. There may not be any signs of it left. But we will look."

"Thank you. Thank all of you."

The men began gathering their papers and heading to the door. Gustav looked shyly at Wanda. She looked expectantly at him. "It's nice seeing you," Gustav said and readied his papers to leave. Wanda looked heartbroken.

As Gustav moved out of earshot, Carla asked, "OK, Wanda, what's the story?"

Wanda's shoulders drooped. "We were in high school. Gustav had a crush on me, and the hunky football quarterback made a pass at me. I went for the pass. Big mistake. The hunk couldn't put two words together, let alone carry on a conversation." Carla understood.

Trying to give Gustav a hint, she asked more loudly than necessary, "Wanda, do you have plans for dinner?" Gustav did not pick up on the hint. He caught up with the other fellows outside. They had a few words and then they all left.

"Looks like it's a girls' night," Carla said as brightly as she could.

"I know a quiet place over on the highway. Want to go there?" Wanda almost begged.

"Do these fellows hang out there?"

"No."

"I'm in. Let me get my purse."

The quiet place was a small dark restaurant next to the Pacific Coast Highway. Parking was across the front and down one side. There was a bar across the back of the main room. Red leather booths lined the front wall and left side. A few tables filled the middle, and a juke box was on the right wall. It was not playing. Wanda ordered a salad, hamburger, French fries, and chocolate milkshake. Carla didn't see a menu so she just said, "Same." The salads and glasses of water were served immediately.

When the salads were finished, Carla could wait no longer. "Wanda, tell me about Gustav. What goes with him? I saw how he looked at you, and you knew exactly how he likes his coffee. You even served only him. What goes?"

"I wish I knew," Wanda lamented, stirring the ice in her water with a straw. "I guess I blew it in high school. He's very shy. Always was. He didn't date much. His family was from Germany, and with the war and McCarthy and all, they pretty much kept to themselves. He wanted to go to college, but his family decided he should work and help his sister through design school. He could make more money with no training than she could, so he could help her. She really couldn't help him at that time."

The waiter brought their hamburgers and French fries. "These are really good," Carla said with a hint of surprise in her voice. "Tell me more about Gustav. Did he get his education?"

"No. His reputation as a good worker kept him busy and employed. It seems he worked himself out of an education by being so good."

"But how did you get to know his coffee preferences?"

Wanda chuckled. "Working in a diner has its perks. Depending on where a job is, work crews will stop by for breakfast. Gustav's crews stopped by pretty often."

"Did he want coffee or you?"

Wanda gave Carla an exasperated look. "Obviously coffee."

"Why didn't you ask him out?"

"Nice girls don't do that!" Wanda replied. Her eyes opened wide.

"Wanda, its 1950. Of course they do."

"This isn't New York, Carla. This is small town USA, and people talk."

"Well, they are saying the wrong things."

"I don't want to talk about this anymore," Wanda warned in a whisper.

"These are good milkshakes," Carla noted, changing the subject, but she was still scheming in her mind.

CHAPTER SEVENTEEN

Work Begins

The sound of road equipment woke Carla. The "sprucing up" had begun. The front loader was clearing debris, making space for the parking lot. Hammers were banging, and plaster was crashing on the floor. Carla quickly dressed and hurried downstairs.

"I'm sorry," Gustav said, "Did we wake you? I thought it would be OK to start. It is after 7:00 a.m."

"It's quite alright. You certainly do get an early start."

"You make hay when the sun shines," Gustav answered with a smile.

"I need a cup of coffee," Carla muttered as she headed to the kitchen.

"We have set up a large pot for the men on the back patio if you want some," Gustav offered. A big smile covered Carla's face.

"I thought you and your crew would be getting breakfast at the diner since we are so close. I mean, Wanda told me you often did that. She was looking forward to serving you," Carla said conspiratorially.

Gustav turned red. Carla hurried to the patio and fixed herself a cup of coffee.

With coffee in hand, Carla moseyed out to the cliff edge. Turning, she remembered she wanted a wrought-iron railing matching the fence rimming the cliff for the front porch. "Juan," she called to get his attention. He came immediately. "I want to serve my guests on the front porch. Can you put a matching wrought-iron railing along the sides and front of it?" Juan looked at the massive adobe-colored house. What should he do? His orders were to do what she asked, but a wrought-iron railing would not look good on the porch.

With a worried look he said, "Miss DuPree, this is a massive house."

"I know that," she replied, not understanding what he was trying to say.

"I will see what I can do," Juan stalled for time.

Gustav's sister, Gertrude, arrived at ten. Carla was immediately impressed with her. She was five foot six or seven and wore a plain dark green straight skirt and short-sleeve pale green blouse. Her shoes were light brown with a wedge heel. Her hair was cut short, and she wore barely any makeup.

Gustav introduced her. She reached out her hand to Carla and said, "I have wanted to see the inside of this place since I first saw it when I was a child. It is a beautiful house."

Carla was sold. Gertie, as everyone called her, was friendly, professional, and knew how to charm a client. Carla was sure they were soulmates. "Welcome to my house. May I show you around or do you want a cup of coffee first?"

"A cup of coffee, please. It will give you a chance to tell me what you have in mind."

"Gertie wants my ideas. This is going to work out wonderfully," Carla thought and smiled to herself.

As they drank their coffee, Carla explained she would like to have the rooms reflect the previous owners. She wanted the Chinese room to honor the Sea Captain. She wanted one of the dining rooms to reflect the gold Prospector, but she wanted the picture of his wife to hang on the wall going up the stairs. "The room with the parquet floor should honor the naturalist. And, of course, the kitchen will be called the 'Bagonski Kitchen,' if he agrees," Carla stressed.

Gertie made notes as Carla talked, nodding every so often. When Carla finished, Gertie asked, "What about the Nuns?"

"Nuns?" Carla repeated.

"Yes. The Nuns ran a home for unwed mothers here. They switched over to retreats a few years back. But they just couldn't make the finances work. They were the owners that sold to Phillip and Dirk."

"Nuns," Carla repeated again and looked around like she was expecting someone to slap her hands with a ruler.

"It's OK," Gertie tried to calm her. "They aren't here anymore and I don't think they ever came back once they left."

"I don't know how to honor Nuns," Carla worried.

"We'll work on that. Right now, show me the rooms."

Carla and Gertie surveyed the first-floor rooms while discussing different ideas, paint colors, and floor coverings and taking measurements. As they headed to the front porch, Carla explained she wanted to serve guests there and had asked Juan to install a wrought-iron railing matching the cliff fence. Gertie wrinkled her brow but didn't say anything.

Gustav and Juan were on the front lawn looking at the house when Carla and Gertie stepped through the door. Gustav was shaking his head side to side and Juan looked worried. Gertie knew immediately what they had been discussing. The two men walked over to greet the ladies. Gertie, a no-nonsense woman, said to Gustav, "Gustav what do you think of a wrought-iron railing on this porch?" Gustav lowered his head. "Juan?" she continued.

Although Carla had regained her trust in herself, she still knew a lot could be learned by listening to others.

"If Miss DuPree wants it," his voice trailed off.

"Carla, this is a big house. A wrought-iron railing will disappear against it. Gustav, what do you think of a wooden railing with some decorative posts?" Gertie demanded.

"I think it will look much nicer. It won't detract from the adobe-colored stucco, and it won't be lost against it either, like a wrought-iron railing would. If you like, I can draw up a few designs," Gustav offered.

Jose nodded in agreement. "I believe he is right, Miss DuPree. But I will do what you want."

Carla pursed her lips. She had so much to learn. "What about screening around the porch?" Carla asked. From the look of horror on their faces, she knew the answer.

Gertie said, "People will come here to see the ocean and enjoy the pleasant mountain breeze. A screen will ruin the experience, I'm afraid."

"These are not the type of people I am use to dealing with," Carla thought. "They always explain their point of view. I think wrought-iron would be more expensive, so they must be giving me honest opinions." She tilted her head toward her right side and smiled. "You are right. I would like to see some wooden railing patterns." Everyone relaxed.

"Back to work!" Gertie ordered.

CHAPTER EIGHTEEN

Lunch With the Girls

The renovations were moving along smoothly. Gertie was a big help, and Wanda was a good sounding board. Carla appreciated them both immensely. It was a Wednesday, the slowest day of the week at the Seaside Diner. So, Wanda only worked a half day. She went to the beach and was about to spread her blanket when she caught a glimpse of the cliff house. She began to think of all the changes taking place there and decided to go see for herself.

Wanda arrived at the cliff house just as Carla and Gertie were finishing their review of the renovation progress. Carla's smile reached from ear to ear when she saw Wanda. "Hi, there! I'm glad you came. I've been thinking it would be fun if the three of us went to lunch together."

Wanda smiled and nodded hello to Gertie. "Sounds good to me. Where do you want to go?"

Gertie stood straight with her head held high. She did not smile. "I would like that," she said stiffly. She was still upset the way Wanda had rejected her brother, Gustav, years before.

"What about that café we went to when we were antiquing?" Carla suggested.

"I know a better place over on the Pacific Coast Highway. Come on. I'll drive," Wanda replied and headed to her car. Carla and Gertie followed.

It was a short drive. Only about fifteen minutes. They talked about the weather and what they wanted to eat. The restaurant was a clean, quiet place with checkered oil-cloth tablecloths and paper napkins. The waitress was friendly and quick. Carla ordered a BLT. Wanda ordered a hamburger with the works, and Gertie ordered a chef salad.

Carla began, "I want to thank you ladies for all the help you have given me with the cliff house. It wouldn't be so far along if it wasn't for you."

"Not a problem," Wanda responded.

"You are good to work with. You listen," Gertie offered. The conversation continued as they noted all who were helping and what good work they were doing. The talking stopped when a work crew of five muscle-bound men entered the restaurant.

"Don't whistle, Wanda," Carla warned.

Wanda gave Carla a you're-a-killjoy look. "Not my type," she snorted.

"All brawn and no brains," Gertie agreed. Then Gertie looked at Carla. "You should go after Phillip. He's your type. Smart and quiet."

"I agree," Wanda chimed in. "Besides, I see the way he looks at you."

"I can't," Carla stuttered. "I have a business arrangement with him."

"A business arrangement!" Wanda was checking out Carla's figure from her head to her toes. "How many customers do you have in this 'business'? Is that what you did back in New York?"

Gertie's eyes widened to the size of ping-pong balls. She pushed herself against the back of her chair. A look of disgust covered her face.

"No, No. Not *that* type of business," Carla hurried to explain.

"Not the same as back in New York?" Wanda pushed the issue.

"I was not in that 'type of business' in New York," Carla was trying to squash her memories of the nights with Winston. She remembered her girlfriends abandoning her. Even if her business relationship with Winston could be interpreted that way after the fact, it didn't start out like that and was not ever meant like that. At least not by her. She did not want Wanda's insinuations to be right or accepted.

Carla quickly continued, "I've made a deal with Phillip to advise me on the restaurant business—menus, kitchen help, food buying, pricing. I don't have any of that kind of experience. I realized that as soon as he showed me around the kitchen the first day I owned the place. I knew I needed help, and it seemed like a good idea at the time."

"Now you're not so sure, are you?" Wanda questioned.

"Wait a minute. I'm not the only single woman here. What about you, Wanda? Why haven't you gone after Gustav? Everyone sees how you look at each other."

"She broke my brother's heart," Gertie more warned than said.

"The timing has just not been right," Wanda mumbled.

"You broke my brother's heart," Gertie said a little stronger.

"And what about you, Gertie? You and Sammy would make a great pair. With your eye for antiques and knowledge for business, you could turn his second-hand store into an antique boutique," Carla said, trying to keep the conversation away from herself.

"When I decide I want a man, I will get one," Gertie declared.

"Me, too," Wanda added.

"Me, three," Carla agreed and they broke into laughter.

The waitress walked over to see if they needed anything else. "Dessert for my friends," Carla announced, waving her hand majestically. Wanda had apple pie à la mode, Gertie had a bowl of fruit, and Carla had a brownie with a scoop of ice cream.

After they devoured the delicious desserts, they returned to the cliff house. Sitting on the front porch, they watched the waves roll in and discussed the current best-selling books and movies. When the sun began to set, Wanda and Gertie left for home. They didn't want to drive the cliff road after dark. Carla stayed on the porch a while longer, thinking about the life she was living, how different it was from her life in New York.

New York was a man-eat-man world. Although she had the best education, including finishing school, she was not prepared for the deceitful ways of the business world. She thought she had landed the perfect job with the perfect boss who complimented her work and gave her gifts. She was too naïve, too trusting. There were clues. The other girls in the office stayed away from her. Her friends drifted away one by one. She made excuses for their behavior. Now she understood. She had no idea then of the price she would pay. But she knew now.

Life was very different here in Otra Vez. People were friendly. They all seemed to know each other and they offered her help and advice whenever she asked. She felt pretty much accepted by the community and was sure that as soon as they saw her prices, she would be accepted by the local businesses. She was not going to be a threat to any of them. As near as she could tell, none of the contractors had cheated her. Her dream restaurant was almost ready to open. She had a few friends. And although Phillip was not her special guy, he was around a lot.

Carla found herself humming on her way to bed. Things were going her way.

CHAPTER NINETEEN

Ready for Business

The first-floor dining rooms were ready within two months, sooner than Carla had expected. Gertie arrived at 10:00 a.m. for a final walk-through with Carla. They started in the north addition, now called the Sea Captain's Room. The Chinese characters in the Sea Captain's Room were indeed happy thoughts, and a friend of Gustav's refreshed the gold paint lettering. A red-and-black low-pile tweed carpet was installed. Painted black chairs were at tables covered with red tablecloths overlaid with white cloths.

The north room, called the Prospector's Room, was painted a pale green and had a dark green-and-brown tweed carpet. Gold brocade floor-length curtains hung at the windows and were tied back with gold rope tassels. The tables were covered with gold cloths overlaid with white. On the large wall next to the U-shaped stairway, gold brocade draperies with twisted silk fringe at the bottom were hung behind the portrait of the Prospector's lady. When Carla came down the stairs in the morning, she sometimes saw herself in the portrait. "Someday," she would tell herself, "I will be surrounded by gold, just like she is."

In the Naturalist's Room, benches with backs, like church pews, lined the walls, leaving the parquet starburst-patterned floor open for dancing. It was unanimously agreed to call this room the Starburst Room. "We should have some sort of sound system for music so we can dance," Carla mused.

"I'll check with some of my music clients," Gertie said, making a note on her list. "I don't think the sound from a phonograph player will be strong enough."

The south room was turned into a waiting room and fitted with well-padded straight chairs and a baby grand piano. They called this room the Music Room to honor the Nuns.

Phillip would not permit Carla to call the kitchen "Bagonski's Kitchen." Although he was very unhappy with his ex-partner, Dirk, he didn't want to rub salt into open wounds. He did agree to call the kitchen Phillip's though. "It could be any Phillip," he reasoned.

Sturdy wooden tables and chairs, painted white, were placed on the front porch. The designs on the backs of the chairs mirrored the railing. The high wrought-iron fence along the cliff edge seemed to fade away in the motion of the waves. Nothing blocked the ocean view. Carla was glad she agreed to the higher fence. Carla and Gertie sat on the porch with a cup of tea reviewing the status of the remaining renovations.

"The flowers and shrubs still look new," Carla worried. Gertie assured her they would grow quickly. The parking lot was finished, and the back patio and grassy area was clean and trimmed. The cliff house was ready.

Carla decided to invite the store owners and town potentates for a grand opening. Offering them a free meal for themselves and a guest might help get their approval, and hopefully, their recommendations to their friends and customers.

She met with Phillip to discuss her plans and menu. "It needs to be elegant," she said. "I don't want them to think I am going to steal business from them. The restaurants in town feed people, and they do it very well. My restaurant is going to be an experience, a destination. I want to serve gourmet meals, like poached salmon, lobster bisque, and beef burgundy on good china with cloth napkins. We already created a sophisticated atmosphere and have magnificent views of the ocean."

Phillip understood only too well. He spent a number of years planning, gathering money, convincing Dirk, and dealing with the bank to make his dream come true. When it all fell apart, he was devastated. He felt everyone was judging him and finding him a failure. It was his parents who lifted him up, showed confidence in him, and helped get financing for his culinary school. Now they lived on the other side of the country, which might as well be the other side of the world. He was on his own now and doing very well. Helping Carla seemed like he was living his dream, but it was no longer his dream. He was past that. Now It was Carla's. And he was more than happy to help her. Mostly because it gave him an excuse to be with her. He liked her attitude and smile, among other things.

"You should limit the menu to three main courses. That will hold down the cost and speed up serving. I suggest a beef, a fish, and a chicken dish."

"That doesn't sound very elegant."

"Call it Surf 'n Turf."

Carla smiled. "You are ingenious."

Phillip smirked. "You will need a waitstaff. Do you have any lined up?"

"I was hoping some of the newer students at your culinary school would like the opportunity," Carla grinned sheepishly. "I am planning on asking Wanda to train them. I know she works in a diner, but I have watched her. She treats people as individuals. She has a way of being patient and pushy at the same time. She handles rowdy customers without them even knowing it. And at the same time, she treats businessmen with respect they really don't deserve."

Phillip was only half listening to Carla. They had a business deal. She was to pay him for restaurant consultation, but he would gladly give it for free. She was a strong-willed woman with a mind of her own. He admired that. And that night on the beach, when the wave dumped her in his arms, she fit perfectly. "I better get going," he said before his purpose for the visit changed. "There is a lot to do in a short time."

Carla watched him rise and walk toward the door. She watched how straight he stood, the long stride of his steps, and remembered the night on the beach. She half wished she had gone home with him, but it was too soon. She needed to know more. "I'll call Wanda," she called after him. He acknowledged with a wave.

Instead, Carla decided it would be better to meet with Wanda face to face. She had been to the cliff house many times. In fact, she had even given Carla advice, which Carla took. She knew the elegant plans Carla had. Wanda liked the diner atmosphere, the type of patrons the diner attracted. She didn't see herself as someone serving in an elegant restaurant.

The diner wasn't busy when Carla arrived. She sat at her favorite table. Wanda came right over. "I've scheduled my grand opening," Carla said softly.

"Mazel tov!" Wanda exclaimed.

"I need your help," Carla practically whispered.

The smile left Wanda's face. She was expecting Carla to ask her to work for her. How could she tell her friend no? "I'm sorry Carla. I can't help you. I've never served in a fancy restaurant, and I really prefer the diner atmosphere."

"I know," Carla agreed. "And don't think I wouldn't love to have you as a server, but that is not what I need from you."

Wanda sat straight up in her chair, wrinkled her forehead, and tipped her head slightly forward. Carla continued, "Wanda I have watched you. You know just when to be sophisticated, or homey, or motherly, or the strictest adult ever. You know when to push someone to order and when to let them take their time. I want you to teach those tricks to my waitstaff. Along with how not to spill coffee on the costumer's lap, and how to keep orders straight, of course. We can schedule a time that's good for you."

Wanda put her hand over her mouth and leaned on the table. The wrinkles were gone, replaced by thinking eyes. "Who did you hire?"

"No one yet. Phillip is getting some of his newer students."

"Who will be there?"

"I'm inviting all the officials and business people in town. I am giving each two tickets for free meals. I want them to understand my restaurant is not in competition with any of them. My restaurant will be too expensive for everyday dining. That is business for the local restaurants. Mine is to be an experience, a destination for special occasions, and for young up-and-comers to impress their business associates."

"I will need to talk to my boss first. I don't want to lose my job. I like it here."

"Please be sure to tell him I won't be his competition. The cliff house is hard to get to. This place is easy."

Wanda was considering the offer. Carla could tell by the look on her face. She didn't want to push too hard and couldn't really think of anything more to sweeten the deal anyway. Deciding it was best to change the subject, she asked. "How's it going with Gustav?"

Wanda turned hot pink. "He's coming for breakfast almost every day."

"Did you ask him out?"

"Of course not!" Wanda whispered. "He's too old-fashioned."

"Tell him you would like to see what he's done with the cliff house."

"He knows I've seen what he's done. He's not stupid."

"Give it a try," Carla said with a wink. She paid her bill, waved goodbye to Wanda, and headed back to the cliff house.

Once home, she walked to the fence by the cliff and looked down on Otra Vez. Her eyes fell on Phillip's house, the large red brick one halfway up the north slope. "You need to know more," she warned herself.

CHAPTER TWENTY

Moving Forward

Wanda agreed to train the waitstaff. Phillip prepared a simple menu and trained his students how to cook it and make the dish look elegant. Invitations went out. Three days before the grand opening, Carla invited those still working on the renovations and landscaping to a run-through. It went smoothly and the staff and chefs relaxed a little. Phillip tweaked the appetizers a bit, and Wanda praised the waitstaff, then she turned to Carla. "You need a new dress," she said.

"I know," Carla sighed. "Wanda, please go shopping with me."

"I'm always ready to go shopping," Wanda's voice sparkled with anticipation. "Grab your bag. I know just the place to go." Carla grabbed her purse and they drove to a small boutique in a town fifteen minutes south of Otra Vez. With Wanda's help, Carla chose a mid-calf-length dress made of light green dotted swiss. It had elbow-length puff sleeves and a scooped neckline edged with lace. Sandals, which Carla had come to love, would complement the dress.

The opening went well. Only a few of those invited did not come. Those who attended said good things about the food and atmosphere. They loved the way the rooms represented the house's history and, by extension, the town's. They thought the prices were outrageous. But since their meals were free, they did not complain. In fact, they were now convinced Carla was not going to steal their customers. Silently they wondered if she was going to have any customers at all, with her prices.

Wanda came with Gustav. It was not Carla's imagination. Wanda had a touch of makeup on, and her mouth was curled up in a little smile. She had her arm wrapped through Gustav's elbow, and her eyes kept returning to Gustav's face. Gustav was standing so stiff, it seemed he might break if a feather bumped him. His smile reached from ear to ear, and there was a hint of red in his cheeks. Wanda winked at Carla. Carla congratulated herself on her match-making abilities.

The only complaint Carla did receive was the difficult drive up the cliff side to the restaurant. Some came by going south then west to the Pacific Coast Highway, which was a long way around. Carla already knew access was a problem, and she was working on it. She wanted to build an incline or cable car to carry customers up the cliff face. The view would be stunning. But it would be too expensive for her to build herself. Besides, the town would benefit from it, so there was no reason for her to bear the full cost. On a smaller scale, she thought a subsidized taxi service would work. She added it to her to-do list. "I can't rush this," she reminded herself. "The town is still not 100 percent sure about me."

At 7:30 a.m. the day after the opening, Carla awoke to the sound of heavy equipment again. Looking out the window, she could see the Garcia's Gardens crew clearing brush from the north side of the barn. Dressing hurriedly and skipping her morning coffee, she ran to the back door. Juan saw her and sprinted toward her. She stepped out onto the patio. "Good morning, Miss DuPree," he said, bowing his head and holding his hat against his chest.

"What are you doing?" Carla snapped.

"Mr. Garcia was very impressed with your dinner. He sends his thanks and congratulations on such a successful opening."

"What are you doing?" Carla snapped again, louder this time.

"Mr. Garcia said you need more parking. He said it would be best on the north side of the barn because it will not ruin the view of the pretty woods."

Carla was livid. How dare he order his crew to work on her property without discussing it with her! This was her property, and she was in charge. No one was going to push her around. He was probably going to charge her double. She knew it. They were all in cahoots to get her money. She could just hear them talking amongst themselves: "Be nice to the lady from New York. Act concerned and take her for every penny she has. When she goes bankrupt, we will be left with a valuable property to attract some real money to Otra Vez." Carla was fuming. She was determined to not let anyone take advantage of her again. New York was still fresh in her mind.

"Mr. Garcia said the beef stroganoff was the best he ever had, and the place was prettier than he ever thought it could be. And I enjoyed the chicken marsala. I hope you are not upset I came with Mr. Garcia."

Carla did a military-style about-face and stepped toward the door. "I'm calling that old man. I'll tell him who's in charge here. Me! That's who. I don't know why he thinks he can just do as he pleases.

Maybe other folks around here allow that, but not me. I own this place and I will decide what is to be done!"

"He's just trying to look out for you," Juan pleaded.

"Yes, look out for how much money he can squeeze out of me."

"No, Miss DuPree. Mr. Garcia would not do that to anyone."

"Except me," Carla snapped and took a second step toward the door. Suddenly the machinery and crew stopped working. One of the men came running across the grass, yelling for Juan.

"It's a grave! It's a grave! We found a grave." Juan took off in the direction the man was pointing. Carla quickly followed. The grave was merely twenty feet past the far corner of the barn.

"It might be the Captain's wife," Juan offered.

"And it might not be," Carla said. "I'll call the sheriff's office." She walked very slowly back to the house. She did not call the old man; she called his good friend, the sheriff. Within a half hour, both men were at the cliff house—the sheriff investigating the grave and Garcia looking for more parking space.

The sheriff cordoned off the area with yellow crime scene tape to protect any evidence that might also be buried with the body until the coroner could come and do testing. Garcia had his crews clear and rehab the driveway that led to the back of the property, explaining that it would give better access to the Pacific Coast Highway. Carla was still unhappy with his takeover attitude.

The grave was the Captain's wife's. Along with the body, the coroner had found some pictures tucked away in the casket. One was of the Captain, his wife, and their little boy. Another was a picture of Otra Vez before the cove was filled in. The pictures were faded and fragile. Carla thought a good artist could replicate them. She added, "find a good artist" to her to-do list. She wanted the pictures to hang in the Sea Captain's Room.

Knowing the story of the Sea Captain's wife, how she had watched and waited for the Captain's return, Carla felt it was only right to keep the body where it had rested for so many years. So, she insisted the bones be returned and re-interred where they had been found. At first she worried the body would turn people away, but the opposite happened. People came in droves. It seemed everyone wanted to see where the "ghost" stayed when she wasn't floating back and forth across the cliff. Carla had Garcia's Gardens build an annual flower garden with two curved concrete benches and a metal marker telling the Captain's wife's story at the spot. She added an inexpensive dessert menu for the ghost seekers. "No sense in missing a money-making opportunity," she laughed with her friends.

Business continued to be good. When it was time for the local high school junior-senior prom, Carla offered the Cliff House (now its formal name) for an after-prom party. The class was only fifty students. A few boys from the school had formed a band, and Carla hired them to play in the Starburst room. She was going to serve buffet-style. Phillip warned her against it. "The boys will do nothing but eat," he said. With his help, she prepared a special menu for the night.

Two days before the prom party, Carla met with her wait-staff and emphasized the importance of maintaining their usual level of service for these teenage guests. She explained that these students were going to be the future customers who would keep them employed, and not to expect big tips. "But not to worry," Carla assured them, "I will make up the difference between your usual take and this special evening's take."

She also made a deal with the local taxi service. If they would transport the prom attendees at a reduced rate, she would include them in her advertising. The parents and school board were overjoyed. To them it was a safe alternative to the usual joy riding and beach partying. They showed their appreciation by frequenting the Cliff House more often (paying full price), and Carla had made an in with the taxi service.

The restaurant was prospering. Carla began think seriously about the amenities she wanted to add: the theater, the incline, the overnight rooms. She opened the dining rooms an hour earlier and closed them an hour later. She had Phillip create a special menu for business and club meetings. The Cliff House reputation was spreading rapidly.

CHAPTER TWENTY-ONE

Shopping

Carla spent her mornings shopping for needed supplies and distributing advertising fliers to shops in nearby towns. It was Wednesday—the day to shop for cleaning supplies and maybe a new pair of pedal pushers. She gathered her list of needed supplies, reached for her keys, and headed out to her car. It was a beautiful day. The sun was shining, but it was not too hot outside. White wispy clouds floated high above the ocean. "If I hurry," she told herself, "I can grab some beach time." Her steps quickened at the thought.

The road from the Cliff House to Otra Vez always made her nervous. She held on to the steering wheel with both hands and kept one foot on the break. She knew it wasn't the best way to drive, but she felt it was the safest, at least for her.

She pulled into a parking space close to the statue at 9:55 a.m. Smiling, she congratulated herself. If the shopping went quickly, and there was no reason it shouldn't, she could get in a good half hour of beach time. She got out of her car with a smile on her face and a bounce in her step. In less than ten minutes, she was at the hardware store gathering the needed supplies.

Carla was headed to the Corner Shop to look for some pedal pushers or slacks, whichever she liked better, when she saw the black limousine beginning to circle the town square. She tensed. "Silly girl," she scolded herself. "This isn't New York. Relax." But it was not so easy. She didn't know who was in the limousine or whom they might represent.

The limousine circled the square and then began to circle it again. It was traveling at an unhurried speed till it got to the hardware store. There it slowed down and drove close to the curb heading toward Carla. Carla quickened her step. The limousine kept pace. She could feel every muscle in her body tighten. She turned to face the limousine. There were two men inside. She couldn't make out the faces. The windows were darkened. She was about to ask what they thought they were doing when she saw old man Garcia headed her way. He had dropped his paper and was bolting across the square, past the statue, with long deliberate strides. His arms were bent at the elbow, and his hands were fists. His face was an angry red. The men in the car turned their heads followed her gaze. Seeing Garcia, they abruptly stepped on the gas and sped off, heading out of town.

Garcia looked at Carla, turned, returned to his bench, gathered his newspaper off the ground, and sat down.

Carla stood still till she could think straight. No one else seemed to notice anything. Once her composure returned, she headed over to Garcia. He kept his newspaper in front of his face. She stopped directly in front of him. "What was that all about?" she demanded.

"What you don't know won't hurt you," he replied.

"That's not true and you know it's not," Carla countered sharply.

"You need some beach time," Garcia said with a soft, even voice. "It will help you relax."

Carla knew he was right but didn't like him having the last word. Besides, she was running out of time. If she didn't get to the beach soon, she wouldn't have time, and she would have to go back to the Cliff House tense and cranky. Clomping her feet so Garcia would be sure to notice, she headed to the beach. It was the right thing to do. By the time she returned to the Cliff House, she was calm, cool, and collected.

CHAPTER TWENTY-TWO

Busy Life

Carla's afternoons and evenings were spent welcoming her guests. Word of the Cliff House was spreading. She hired an office assistant and a host. Her professional life was beyond her imagined success. Her personal life, however, was slim to nothing.

Carla didn't miss a personal life. Once she graduated from college and started working, her personal life was nothing to envy. She had been taken in and used by her boss, Winston. Her colleagues at work avoided her once they found out. Her college and high school friends turned the other way when they saw her. Even her more compassionate friends faded away. Her life was different now, and she had no desire to turn back, even though life now was extremely hard and busy. Plus, she had no time for herself.

One look in the mirror told her she had to make time for at least a haircut. Customers saw her every day, and she could not afford to look unkempt. When she finished her morning coffee, she headed to the Clips & Curls.

The old man, Garcia, was sitting in his usual place on the bench facing the statue of Mr. Richardson in the park. Carla studied him for a few moments before she got out of her car. "We're really pretty much alike," she thought, "Both successful and alone."

Gloria, the beautician, was ready for her. "How are you, Carla? Boy, you really need a cut."

"Do I ever!" Carla agreed. There was more unimportant chit-chat, then the conversation drifted off. "Gloria," Carla ventured, "What do you know about old man Garcia?"

"He's a wonderful man," Gloria said matter-of-factly.

"What's his story?"

"Well, I wasn't here at the time, you know. I'm not that old," Gloria paused briefly. "I was told he and some others were brought here by Mr. Richardson to fill in the cove. You know the cove used to be much smaller and lower." Carla nodded. "Well, the lower stores and houses were always flooding with any storm tide. So Mr. Richardson decided to fill in the cove like New York City and Baltimore and other places had done. So, as I said, he brought Mr. Garcia and others in to do the work. But Mr. Richardson didn't really have the know-how. They started the construction and the materials weren't strong enough and there wasn't enough of them. Mr. Garcia told Mr. Richardson this. Mr. Richardson thought Mr. Garcia was, pardon the expression, just a dumbass kid, and told him to do as he was told. Mr. Garcia explained the problem to the other workers and they decided to strike. Mr. Richardson was furious. He threatened to fire all of them. Of course the other workers had families they needed to feed, so they went back to work. Mr. Garcia warned them again. But they said they had no choice. So Mr. Garcia went back to work with them.

"Now you know Otra Vez is a very beautiful beach, and the young girls like to sunbathe there—including Mr. Richardson's daughter, Anna. Word was that Mr. Richardson was a very controlling man and she was a very rebellious daughter. She had heard her father complain about Mr. Garcia. She knew it would rankle her father if Mr. Garcia made eyes at her. What she didn't count on was falling in love with Mr. Garcia.

"Well, she made eyes. Mr. Garcia didn't know who she was, only that her name was Anna. A romance blossomed and went further than it should have. She became with child, if you know what I mean, and her father sent her to live with the Nuns in the Cliff House.

"She didn't tell Mr. Garcia. She only said she didn't want to see him anymore. Mr. Garcia wasn't surprised. After all, she was obviously a higher class than him.

"About then, the cove structure gave way, swamping the workers. Mr. Garcia personally pulled four other men out. Two saved themselves and one drowned. Mr. Richardson made a phony apology to Mr. Garcia and gave him a two-year scholarship to an agricultural school somewhere in southern California. He said it was in appreciation for saving the four men. It turns out his motive was to get rid of Mr. Garcia. Mr. Garcia didn't learn about the baby till three years later."

"How sad."

"It was three years later, like I said, when Mr. Garcia came back. He had an education now and felt worthy to date Anna. He asked around about her and learned she was Mr. Richardson's daughter and had a baby. Now the scholarship made sense. He went to Mr. Richardson and demanded to see Anna. But Anna didn't want to see him. She wasn't herself anymore. She didn't go to the beach, or anywhere for that matter. She had grown weak and sullen. Mr. Garcia vowed to bury Mr. Richardson. And he did so by becoming a great man. He built that white stucco house opposite and five feet higher than Richardson's red brick one. The one Phillip Bagonski lives in now. Garcia placed the windows so he could see Anna over the wall, but Richardson couldn't see him. He sits by Richardson's statue every day.

"It looks like he's mocking Richardson, but he says it keeps him humble. Mr. Garcia has succeeded more than Richardson ever expected.

"Anna died about ten years ago. Richardson left Otra Vez full of sorrow. Otra Vez is a small town, Carla. Here you treat people right."

Carla didn't know if she had been warned or given advice. Either way, it was worth knowing. She left the salon and headed through the park to her car. When she got to the statue of Richardson, she stopped and kicked him in the shin, hurting her toe. She took her shoe off and rubbed her foot. Mr. Garcia laughed. Carla put her head down and mumbled, "I don't care. He deserved it."

CHAPTER TWENTY-THREE

Moving On

The Cliff House clientele continued to grow, with more and more guests coming from out of town. The only payment methods were cash and checks. The large amount of cash was beginning to make Carla nervous, and with more out-of-town guests, she feared more bad checks. No one in Otra Vez would give her a bad check; they watched their reputations carefully. Still, there were a lot of out-of-town guests who she didn't know personally.

Shortly before Carla left New York in 1950, she learned about the new Diners Club International system for charging meals at restaurants. Restaurants would accept the Diners Club membership card as a customer's payment and send a bill to the Diners Club. Diners Club would then reimburse the restaurant. Carla called Ron Gunderson, her friend and financial advisor in New York, and asked him to check it out. He said he would and would get back to her. Her plan was to impress the other merchants in town with her business shrewdness, thereby gaining their respect. She reasoned that respect would translate into support when she approached them with a plan to build an incline from Otra Vez to the Cliff House.

Ron learned a competing venture, Dine and Sign, was active in California. He forwarded Carla's information to them; they agreed to contact her. This was good news for Carla. She was getting smothered with day-to-day duties. The office assistant and host she had hired helped immensely; still, not having to chase after bad checks would free more time. Time she could put toward starting her other dreams.

Unlike Phillip and his partner, Dirk Jenkins, who lost their dream when Dirk could no longer pay his share and Phillip could not cover both. Although Phillip did not own his Cliff House dream, he was still enjoying it vicariously through Carla. His fallback dream, the culinary school, was thriving, thanks in great part to the Cliff House.

Dirk had gone back to the sea as a worker on a cruise ship. He started in the kitchen as a helper, advanced to cabin boy, then server, and finally as Maître d' in the dining room. The work was hard and the days were long. Yet the skills he learned in pacifying and charming customers were invaluable. He had naturally good looks—tall, dark, and handsome, as they say.

When Dirk's contract with the cruise ship company was over, he returned to Otra Vez. When he heard about the changes at the Cliff House, the first thing he did was visit Phillip. "I see there have been a few changes at the Cliff House," he began after the obligatory catch-up talk.

Phillip was happy to see Dirk until the subject of the Cliff House came up. "Yes," Phillip answered brusquely. He was immediately suspicious of where Dirk was going with this. Phillip didn't want anyone messing up his "arrangement" with Carla.

"I hear there's a pretty young girl running it," Dirk continued with a glint in his eye.

Phillip's eyes narrowed. The veins in his neck started to bulge. His heart was pounding. "You stay away from her," he warned menacingly.

"Have you put a claim on her?" Dirk asked innocently.

"Not exactly," Phillip had to admit. "But you stay away. Something happened back in New York. I don't know what. But she's fragile. So you just stay away."

"You don't have a claim on her, so she's free for the picking."

Phillip jumped out of his seat and lunged toward Dirk. "Slow down, buddy," Dirk said, stepping back and holding his hands out for protection. "That's the way it is. No claim, no say."

Phillip looked at the floor.

Dirk stood and reached out his right hand to Phillip. "May the best man win," he said with a devious smile. Phillip did not shake his hand. Dirk snickered and left.

Phillip was shaken. His anger and disappointment in Dirk over the restaurant had faded. But Dirk's conversation left him uneasy. He liked what he had going. It wasn't the money. He made enough off the school to live handsomely. It was the private talks with Carla he enjoyed. The quiet time they shared watching the ocean. The hopes and dreams they confided in each other. It was hard for him to make friends. Acquaintances, yes; friends, no. He was not the outgoing, boisterous, life-of-the-party type like Dirk. He felt threatened.

Dirk made a few more stops around town, renewing old acquaintances and gathering as much gossip as possible. At four o'clock he headed to the Cliff House. He did not see Carla when he entered, but the staff saw him and recognized him. He was greeted warmly and seated with a view of the ocean.

The host hurriedly found Carla and told her Dirk Jenkins was in the Sea Captain's Room.

Carla recognized the name immediately. "Well, lead me to him," she said decisively. Carla had never inquired about Dirk. She had no idea what he looked like or what type of a man he was. She understood he had paid his share as long as he could, so she presumed he had as much interest in the Cliff House as Phillip. She was on guard, but when she met him, her knees went weak. He was beautiful and he was smiling at her. "Welcome, Mr. Jenkins," she said, trying to appear professional.

"Call me Dirk. What you have done with this place is nothing short of miraculous. I don't think Phillip and I could have done anything this magnificent." He was laying it on thick.

"Thank you. Have you ordered yet?"

"Yes. Here comes my meal now."

"Brandon, when Mr. Jenkins finishes his dessert, please find me. I want to show him around the Cliff House. If you want me to, Dirk."

"I would love it." When Dirk finished his meal, he had to admit it was incredible. Better than any served on the cruise ship, and that was saying something. He did notice a few things that could be improved, such as the printed menu and kitchen noise. That would be his "in."

"Are you ready?" Carla asked as she signed his bill.

"After a meal like that, I'm ready for anything," Dirk winked at Carla and left a nice tip for the waiter. Previous waiters always seemed to leave nice tips.

Carla led him to the front door, pointing out the view of the ocean ahead and the redwoods through the big window behind. "Heart and Soul," she said and smiled. They walked across the porch, nodding at the guests and onto the front lawn. Dirk commented on the new wrought-iron fence and the outstanding landscaping. "Garcia's Gardens," Carla confessed. They circled around to the back and briefly explored the barn. "I have a dream of turning this into a theater," Carla confided to Dirk.

As they were exiting the barn, Dirk saw Phillip drive up in the school's van. He was coming to take his students home. The opportunity was too much for Dirk to pass up. He reached down, took Carla's hand in his, and turned so Phillip could see, but not hear, him telling Carla how much he enjoyed the evening. Phillip walked over to them. Dirk said, "She's quite a lady."

It was too much for Phillip. He had been using his "business arrangement" with Carla to woo her in his own quiet way. Unfounded thoughts raced through his head: "Did he kiss her? Did she kiss him? Where have they been? Who does Dirk think he is? Does he think he can just waltz back here, unannounced, and move in on my territory? He doesn't deserve Carla. She's too good for him. She's too much of a lady. He better take his hands off her." Dirk winked at Carla.

Incensed, Phillip hauled off and hit Dirk on the chin and followed with a punch to the stomach. Dirk doubled over. His lip started to bleed. He was beyond surprised. He intended to rile Phillip, but did not expect this reaction. He thought Phillip would make a stand for Carla. Carla was too dumbfounded to move. Phillip took a step in Dirk's direction. Dirk backed up, losing his balance and falling on his behind.

"Stop! Stop!" Carla shouted as she tried to push Phillip away. By now the guests were all in a circle around them. "Phillip, you need to get your students home. Now! Dirk, you may stay in the upstairs south room if you want. That looks like a nasty bruise. We better put ice on it."

"We didn't improve that room," Dirk said just to aggravate Phillip.

"I know," Carla replied. "You didn't improve the north room either. We need to get that ice."

Phillip's students gathered their gear. Dirk grinned at Phillip. Phillip stood taller than he was and clenched his fists.

"Sonny, fighting is not the way to win your lady-love," said a sweet elderly lady who had watched the entire scene. "It's as obvious as the day is long. And my dinner was the best I ever had," she added, before being hurried off by her children.

The next day, two deliveries arrived from Garcia's Gardens. One was an arrangement of twenty-four yellow roses from Dirk. The other was a red rose bush in a container ready to be planted from Phillip. Carla asked Juan to plant the bush by the front fence so she could see it from all the dining rooms.

CHAPTER TWENTY-FOUR

More Help

"Dirk," Carla began at lunch the day after the fight, and after the flower deliveries, "I want to apologize. I know you had dreams for this place, and you put a lot of money into it."

"No need to apologize, Carla. I deliberately baited Phillip. I could see he has a good thing going here. I saw how you looked at him. Then I saw his name on the kitchen door, and mine nowhere. Well, I guess jealously took over. It was uncool of me, as the kids would say. And I'm sorry. I was way out of line."

"I wanted to call it Bagonski's Kitchen. Phillip wouldn't allow it because of you. He said you both worked hard on the kitchen and you both lost. He said Phillip could be any Phillip and not such an affront to you."

Dirk's shoulders dropped. His face reddened. "I had no idea," he mumbled.

"Can we put it behind us?" Carla asked. "Can Phillip?"

"I can. We'll probably have to give Phillip some time before he'll trust me again," Dirk said seriously.

"Phillip has been immensely helpful to me, and I still want his help. If you want to stay, we have to find a way to make this work."

"Understood. I think you have done a good job with this place. However, I do have a few suggestions for improvements, beginning with the printed menus."

Carla's ears perked up. She knew some improvements were needed. She clearly didn't know where to begin. Besides, her time was completely taken up with the day-to-day operations. "So you would be willing to help me, without decking Phillip every time you see him?" Carla teased.

"With his help," Dirk, always the smooth talker, replied.

"What's first?" Carla asked.

"The menus, then the barn. I have a few contacts with entertainers from the ship. I think we could turn the barn into your theater relatively easily, and, with the help of my contacts, maybe get it to pay for itself."

Carla's heart skipped a beat. This was what she wanted. This was the dream she had told Ron when she first told him to send her money. "It would be my dream come true," she exclaimed, grinning up at Dirk. "Do you really think we can do this?" With the amount of hope shining in her eyes, there was no way Dirk could say no. "When do we start?" she asked eagerly.

"They say the best time to start a project is always now," Dirk had caught the bug. And no wonder—Carla's enthusiasm was contagious.

"I think we should call Sammy at the antique shop and Gertie, my decorator, to check out the stuff stored in the barn. I don't know junk from valuables. I'll call them now. And maybe Gustav can give us names of men who will help."

"And I'll call my contacts. If they can't come, maybe they will know someone who will." It was hard to tell who was more excited, Carla or Dirk.

Every day Phillip delivered his student chefs and waiters and picked them up to take them home as usual. Each time Dirk was nearby. A week went by and Phillip still wouldn't or couldn't be civil to Dirk. It was starting to cause tension. Dirk decided to take matters in his own hands and went to confront Phillip at his culinary school, figuring there would be less of a chance of another outburst there.

Dirk arrived unannounced and asked the secretary to tell Phillip he was there. She did. Dirk could hear Phillip yell clear out in the reception office. The stunned secretary came out and with a shaky voice said, "I'm sorry, Mr. Bagonski can't see you right now."

"I understand," Dirk replied and marched straight to Phillip's office and burst in. "We're going to settle this right now," he said with a no-discussion attitude. "Sit down and listen to me. I handled the situation badly. You didn't react like I expected. I thought you would make a stand for Carla by telling me to back off. Not by decking me. What's with you?"

"It's all kind of mixed up," Phillip muttered, his eyes searching the room for answers. "I thought helping with the menu would give me a chance to get to know Carla. You know? Instead it turned into a business deal and I don't know how to change it to friendship."

"First off, do you want a friend or something more? You need to decide what you want."

Phillip hesitated, trying to decide how much to admit. Finally he said, "I want more."

"Then you have to go for it before someone else does. I'm not going to compete with you. But I can't stop all the other guys."

Phillip's face softened. His shoulders drooped. He twisted his mouth and took a little breath. "You've been around more than me. What should I do?"

"How is this working for you financially?'

"I haven't billed her for any of my time. Only for the students."

"So the worst that could happen is you would make money off of her?"

"Don't say it like that! I don't want to make money off her. I want…" Phillip's voice trailed off.

"My suggestion is you start to date her. Take her to the movies, or a museum, or a walk on the beach."

Phillip remembered the kiss on the forehead he gave her the night they walked on the beach. "Did that. Almost blew the whole thing."

"Well take her someplace new, someplace she hasn't been, someplace you like. Find out what she likes to do. Maybe you can make a connection with her interests. And don't take too long. She's a peach and ripe for the picking."

With that, Dirk got up and walked out of Phillip's office, nodded to the secretaries, and left.

CHAPTER TWENTY-FIVE

Theater

At Carla's urging, Dirk contacted his theater acquaintances in Los Angeles and Hollywood. This was a dream of Carla's and she was anxious to get started.

Dirk told his acquaintances, Sabastian and Douglas, the plan and his concerns about the size of the barn and access to the property. Both were legitimate concerns, his contacts agreed. Still, Sabastian and Douglas were both intrigued with the idea and said they would come to check out the place. Dirk gave them directions coming up the Pacific Coast Highway and in through the cleared driveway past the redwoods.

They arrived at the Cliff House a little before noon. Sabastian looked annoyed, like he was wasting his time. Douglas sashayed across the grass to the house.

Considering himself a director, Sabastian was conservatively dressed in a white shirt and suspenders holding black pleated trousers up over his portly stomach. The thinning of his brown hair was made obvious by combing the left side over the top of his balding head.

Douglas fancied himself an actor and agent. He wore dark pleated trousers with the bottom of the legs folded and turned up in the pegged pants style, a pale green shirt with blousy sleeves, and a dark green silk scarf tucked at the neck. He was average height. His dark hair was brushed into a wave on the top of his head and combed tight against the sides. His thin straight mustache looked like a pencil line. He walked with his nose in the air and held a cigarette in a holder in his right hand. The cigarette was never lit.

Sabastian and Douglas were impressed with the redwoods leading onto the Cliff House property. They gave a passing glance and nod at the barn as they headed to the back entrance of the Cliff House. When they walked through the hallway to the front doors and saw the beautiful ocean view, they were hooked. "You have to make the barn work," they said with dollar signs flashing in their eyes. "This place will be a gold mine."

At that, Carla chuckled as she thought, "Otra Vez, another time. The place has returned to its beginnings. The Prospector must have left some of his golden touch."

"Have you seen inside the barn?" Carla asked. "Is it big enough? Do you really think people will drive this far for an off-Broadway show?" Carla was full of questions. This was a big step, and she didn't know the business or architecture.

"No, yes, yes," Sabastian answered. "I want to see the inside, but it is past lunchtime and, if possible, I would like something to eat." Sabastian was a big man.

"Of course. I should have offered you lunch," Dirk replied quickly. "It's just that I'm so excited, I forgot about eating."

After a very hearty lunch, Sabastian and Douglas went off by themselves to look at the barn. "Douglas," Sabastian started, "This place could be exactly what we need to try out new talent. We could invite agents and the critics we want. It's too far to travel for run-of-the-mill shows, but not for special invites."

"I agree. But how do we get to the money? Dirk we can work. But that Carla is no dummy. She has made this place what it is. She is not going to fall for sweet talk or double talk," Douglas schemed.

"The money will come from the shows. We'll have to be careful how any contracts are worded so we get a hefty cut of the door. They will probably want rent for the space, which we can bargain to keep low by offering a small percentage of the profits instead. We can control the production costs, inflating them as necessary, to keep the profits small. It shouldn't be too hard. These are not theater-savvy people. We'll have to stay in close contact to gain their trust."

"What do you think of the space?" Dirk called as he entered the barn.

Douglas and Sabastian abruptly stopped talking and turned quickly toward Dirk. "It's great," Sabastian said.

"Yes," added Douglas. "I would suggest, though, turning the second floor into dressing and sleeping rooms for the artists. They don't need much, only a cot, mirror, and dressing table."

"I thought having a high ceiling would be better for sound," Dirk ventured.

"Depends on your sound system. A room this size won't need much." Sabastian looked around as he talked.

"I will discuss your suggestions with Carla. Thanks for coming. I know it was quite a hike."

"How do you get to the ocean from here?" Douglas asked.

"There is a road next to the south side of the property that leads down into Otra Vez. It's pretty curvy and steep. But there are few accidents. Come, I'll show you." Dirk led the two men to the front wrought-iron fence and pointed out the road. "When you get to the beach, you can turn south and drive along the coast back to L.A."

"Looks like an interesting place down there," Douglas commented.

"You're driving," Sabastian reminded him.

"Let's go for it," Douglas declared.

Carla came out when they were ready to leave. "Thank you, gentlemen, for coming. I know you have busy schedules, and I really appreciate you taking the time to look at our out-of-the-way place."

Sabastian reached out and shook her hand. "You have a great opportunity here. I will be happy to help you in any way I can."

Douglas followed suit and gave her a limp handshake. "I'll be keeping in touch," he said with so much sugar it felt sticky.

That same evening, Dirk and Carla met over a cup of coffee at the Seaside Diner to discuss the men's suggestions. Carla was hesitant. "I don't know much about buildings. I mean how they are built. And I know less about building regulations. I think your two friends are knowledgeable about the theater. And I think their opinion regarding that is important and useful. Still, I think I need to call Walter Ivenson from Pacific Coast Architects. He was highly recommended and gave me good advice when I started remodeling. Gustav knew him. They had worked together before. I'll call him tomorrow."

"I agree. Sabastian and Douglas did seem to know about the entertainment business. But when I approached them in the barn, they stopped talking. I think we need to proceed with caution." Carla agreed. She had experience with people talking secretly.

The next morning Carla called Walt and told him of the plans to start on the theater. "Carla, as you know, there are fire and health codes for buildings used by the public. Since previous owners also opened for public gatherings, the Cliff House only needed minor updates to meet those codes. The barn will be different. I'll call Gustav to set up an appointment to come for an inspection." Walt was excited. He liked the Cliff House and he enjoyed a challenge, which he expected the barn to be.

A few days later Walt Ivenson and Gustav inspected the building and determined where mandatory restrooms could be placed. They agreed making actors' dressing rooms on the second floor was a good idea. They did call Sabastian to determine the ideal size for the stage and backstage areas. It was going to be a big job, too big for Gustav to handle by himself. So Walt introduced another contractor. But Carla insisted Gustav was to be the head contractor. Secretly she hoped it would give Wanda and Gustav more time together, at least for breakfast.

Dirk and Carla reviewed the plans with Phillip as they developed. Phillip was coming around more often. He managed to rearrange his schedule at his culinary school to give him time to date Carla on Mondays, the one day of the week the restaurant was closed. Carla managed to find more and more questions regarding the menus, cooking staff, and waitstaff in order to spend extra time with Phillip. Since this was one-on-one time with Phillip, she was able to ask his impression of the theater project without involving Dirk. It wasn't that she didn't trust Dirk. She did. She simply wanted to make sure she wasn't making business decisions based on a dream. Besides, she wasn't completely comfortable with Douglas and Sabastian. Especially Douglas.

CHAPTER TWENTY-SIX

Same Old, Same Old

Carla had a television set in her private quarters, one of the few in Otra Vez. She did not want it where her clientele could see or hear it. "The war between North and South Korea or the advances being made on the hydrogen bomb will not encourage anyone to buy meals at my prices," she believed. On evenings when business was slow, she sometimes allowed the staff, usually Sissy, to provide entertainment by singing or playing the piano in the Music Room.

Sissy, a waitress and the daughter of Carla's office assistant, was almost eighteen years old, with only church choir voice training. Folks often told her she should go to Hollywood because of her beautiful voice and attractive good looks. Her hair was long, blond, and wavy. Her eyes sparkled, and she had a ready laugh that could make even the sourest creature smile. She was friendly by nature and as naïve as they come.

Douglas began showing up on a weekly basis to watch the progress on the theater. Without ever mentioning any names, he would say, "I have a number of clients wanting to book time here," giving the impression he was a big deal in Hollywood. Since everyone was eager for the theater to open, his big talk made it easy for him to become overly friendly with the Cliff House staff. Dirk noticed, but excused it as just "Hollywood's" way.

It was a slow evening. Sissy was singing and Tommy was playing along at the piano. Douglas was there. The staff had become accustomed to seeing Douglas and did not pay any attention to him. He saw an opportunity and made his move. He ensnared Sissy and began his sweet talk. It was a dream come true for Sissy. A big Hollywood somebody was telling her she was great, she had potential, and he could make her a star.

For him, it was easy to entice Sissy upstairs to Dirk's room to "discuss her future."

Sissy was so flattered she didn't realize what she was getting herself into. Some of the kitchen staff saw Sissy going upstairs with Douglas. They discussed what they should do; was it any of their business? Her mother was Miss DuPree's assistant. Should they tell her? They were pretty sure Douglas was offering Sissy a Hollywood job. If they interfered, would they be ruining her future? They decided to call Phillip.

As soon as they told Phillip Sissy was upstairs with Douglas, the phone went dead. Phillip was on his way.

While mingling with the customers, Carla noticed a change in the staff's attitude. They all looked a little scared and turned away from her, and the stairs. Carla looked up the stairs and knew instinctively what was going on.

She charged up the stairs. Her lips were pressed tight. Her eyes were glaring. Smoke could almost be seen coming from her ears. Her back was straight. Her feet hit the steps hard. She stopped at the door to the room Dirk was living in. She heard a voice. It wasn't Dirk's. She hesitated.

"You have everything Hollywood is looking for. Plus, you have an amazing stage presence," the voice said. Carla knew who it was: Douglas. She could hear him move closer to Sissy. "Let me see you," the voice continued.

New York flooded Carla's mind. She could feel Winston's soft caresses on her arms and back. Now they felt like maggots crawling over her skin. She could hear the promises he made to her. They were lies. He told her she was talented and gave her gifts. She thought they were gifts of love. But he was enticing her to break the law. They were payoffs. She could feel his warm breath on her neck, which had made her melt. Now it turned her to ice. She banged on the door. It flew open. Sissy was standing by the window holding her blouse closed. Douglas turned to Carla.

"Why, hello Carla. What can I do for you?" A smiling Douglas said so sweetly it was a wonder the bees didn't attack him.

"How dare you!!" Carla yelled. "How dare you take advantage of so young a girl. Who do you think you are, and where do you think you are? This is not some filthy brothel in Hollywood. This is a fine establishment that has extended courtesy to you. Undeserved courtesy. Sissy, go to my office now!"

"I'm sorry," Sissy began.

"Now! Go!" Carla shouted.

Douglas held his hands out with palms up. "I think there is a misunderstanding here," he said with a slanted smile.

"You are despicable. I'm sorry I ever laid eyes on you. Your kind takes advantage of others with no regrets, no apologies, no remorse. You have no conscience. No soul. You are lower than a snake."

"Now Carla…"

"Get out! Get out of my house. Get off my property and never, never come back." Carla turned, rushed out of the room, and headed straight to her living quarters down the hall. Picking up the phone, she pounded out Gustav's phone number.

"Hello," Gustav answered in his usual gentle voice.

"This is Carla DuPree. I want you to come as soon as you can and demolish the south bedroom on the second floor. I want everything out—furniture, wallpaper, cupboards, curtains. Everything."

"Hello?" Gustav repeated, not believing what he had heard.

"As soon as possible. Everything," Carla demanded sharply and slammed down the phone.

She reached for the doorknob on her room's door. She was about to open it when the nightstand next to her bed caught her eye. She walked to it with deliberate steps, opened the small top drawer, and seized the gun lying there. Turning sharply, she hurried out the door. "He better be gone," she murmured.

He was not.

"I told you to get out," she screamed.

A crowd of staff and customers was gathered at the foot of the stairs and outside the backdoor directly below Dirk's bedroom window. Phillip's car skidded to a stop at the edge of the parking lot. He saw the crowd, jumped out, and hurried inside. Exiting the barn, Dirk saw the crowd and grasped something was wrong. He ran, trying to catch up with Phillip. Phillip stopped outside the bedroom door to regain his composure.

"Now, little lady," Douglas commenced in a condescending tone. It was too much.

"I'm not a little lady. Unlike you, I'm a successful business person in spite of your kind." Carla pulled the gun from her pocket. "You owe me an apology and you owe Sissy an apology and an explanation of how rotten you and your kind are."

"Well," Douglas began mumbling, when Carla heard a sound behind her. Surprised, she spun toward the door. As she turned, the gun went off. Douglas screamed. Phillip burst into the room. Carla looked at Douglas and saw blood running down his arm.

"Look what you did!" Douglas screamed as he grabbed his bleeding arm.

Carla's eyes glazed over. Her mind whirled. She was expecting to see Winston. But it was Douglas. She started to lower the gun, but her finger twitched and she shot Douglas again, this time in the leg. He fell to the floor, writhing in pain. Carla started to laugh. "Serves you right."

"Carla," Phillip said in a soft low voice. "Where did you get the gun?" He walked toward her slowly as he talked. Carla tilted her head to the right. Phillip reached out, took the gun from her hand, and gave it to Dirk.

"Someone help me," Douglas called out. No one answered.

The sheriff jumped when the phone rang. Otra Vez is a quiet little town, and the sheriff's phone rarely rang. "Carla shot the guy," the voice on the phone shouted. The sheriff's breath caught in his throat. Bloodshed! Gangster warfare! It was what he had feared when he first saw her New York license plate. Had he let his guard down? Like everyone else in town, he had come to like Carla. She was bringing badly needed business to the town. But at what price? He strapped on his pistol and headed to the Cliff House.

Word about trouble at the Cliff House had already spread, and the road from Otra Vez to the Cliff House was blocked by traffic. The sheriff had to call the nearest town, Summit, on the Pacific Coast Highway for backup. A call went out for an ambulance, and Douglas was taken to the hospital in the town just south of Otra Vez.

Carla was arrested and taken to the single-cell holding jail in Otra Vez. "I'll be there as soon as I can," Phillip assured Carla right before the police car pulled away.

Phillip hurried to the jail and stayed as close as he could to Carla. Dirk did his best to calm the staff. Carla was refused bail because the sheriff knew the town's people would make it impossible to find her. It seemed everyone liked her, and she had been good for the business community.

Carla's one phone call was to Ron Gunderson in New York.

It was 5:30 a.m. in New York when Ron Gunderson's home phone rang. "Hello."

"Ron?"

"Yes. Carla?"

"Yes." Her voice was weak.

"What's the matter?" Ron spoke as he tried to rush the sleep from his mind. Glancing at the clock he calculated it was only 2:30 a.m. in California. "Where are you?"

"In jail. I need a lawyer."

"What for?"

"I shot a man." Carla's voice got softer. "Twice." Ron couldn't speak. He never expected anything like this from Carla. "Are you still there?" Carla's voice trembled.

"I'm here. Is he dead?" Ron didn't really want to know if he was.

"No. He's in the hospital."

"I'm on my way." Ron pulled on his pants and headed to the door, dragging the phone with him.

"I need a lawyer, Ron. No offense, but you are a financial expert. I don't think money will get me out of this mess."

"You are a client of our firm, Carla. Our California office has lawyers. I will call them. But you will also need a friend. I'm coming."

"The sheriff says I have too many of them. That's his excuse for not giving me bail."

No bail. This sounded very bad. "I'm on my way, Carla. Don't say anything to anyone."

CHAPTER TWENTY-SEVEN

The Lawyer

Time was of the essence. The California office of Richmann and Stockard, Ron's firm, would not be open for at least another three hours. By that time, Ron hoped to be on a plane heading west. It would be a minimum eight hours before he could get there. He couldn't wait that long. He called the California office and left a message stating a client was in jail. Then he left a message for his secretary telling her Carla was in jail in Otra Vez and to give the California office the information when they called. With his briefcase and queasy stomach, he took his seat on the plane.

Ron's reaction made Carla realize she was in serious trouble. The problems in New York had been serious. Still, there was no clear trail to tie Carla to any wrongdoing. This time, though, a man had been shot, twice. And she had done the shooting.

Now, she had to decide how much to confide in the lawyer Ron was sending. "I need his sympathy," she reasoned. "I have to explain myself, but not give too much information. I will have to be very careful with what I say. I don't want Winston or his accomplices hearing about this. I don't want to lose the life I have built here."

Attorney James Mason from the California office of Richmann and Stockard was an older gentleman. Over the years, most of his cases involved money and wills. He had grown more cynical and impatient with each case. Ron's secretary didn't give him much information, because all she knew was Carla's name and town. He sat for a while just looking at her name, Carla DuPree, and the town, Otra Vez. He was familiar with Otra Vez. A nice, quiet beach town. He called the Otra Vez sheriff and inquired about Carla.

"She shot a man twice. Once in the shoulder and once in the leg. Claims it was an accident. According to witnesses, the man was hitting on one of Carla's young waitresses," the sheriff told him, trying not to divulge too much information.

James Mason almost started to salivate. Finally, a case that had some moral teeth to it. "Is he dead?"

"No. He's in the hospital in Sea Port."

"Tell Carla I'm her attorney and not to speak to anyone." Mason grabbed his jacket, told his secretary he was taking the case, and headed to Otra Vez jail.

Mason always wore a dark blue suit with a starched white shirt and small print necktie. Glancing around Otra Vez, he decided a more casual look would make him more acceptable to the locals, and therefore, it would be easier to get information. He put his necktie in his pocket and slung his jacket over his shoulder before entering the sheriff's office.

The sheriff led Mason to a private visitation room and brought Carla to him. He was surprised when he saw her. She was just a few years older than his daughter. Carla looked scared to death, but still maintained her professionalism and poise the way she had been taught at finishing school. She politely held out her right hand and introduced herself. "Hello, I'm Carla DuPree. I understand you are from Richmann and Stockard and have agreed to represent me."

"That is correct." Mason paused. "How old are you?" he asked, shocking both himself and Carla.

"What does it matter?" Carla asked. She could feel doubts and fears about this lawyer creeping up her spine.

"All the New York office told me was your name and town. All I know about the incident is what the sheriff told me. I did some checking on you before I left the office and learned you own the Cliff House where the incident took place. You do not look like the person I conjured in my mind. I thought you would be much older." He paused. "I have a daughter about your age. That brings this case home."

"Does that mean you do not want to represent me?" Carla ask maintaining her calm appearance and passive voice.

"Not at all. Tell me what happened. Start with where you got the gun?"

"Winston gave it to me."

"Who is Winston?"

"When I graduated from college, I began working for Winston. He was a partner of the firm."

"What kind of business was it?"

"It was a money-lending business. I know the firm took advantage of borrowers. They charged them extra fees to pad their own pockets. I was not involved directly with that."

"A money-lending business that cheated its customers and gave you a gun. I think you better start at the beginning."

"At first I was just Winston's secretary. He was very nice to me, gave me lots of compliments. First on my work, then on my appearance. He took me to fine restaurants. Soon Winston began asking me to deliver packages to his apartment. I thought nothing of it at the time. Soon we were meeting at his apartment, and he was very friendly, if you know what I mean."

Mason nodded. "Continue."

"Well, he started giving me gifts, expensive gifts. Which I kept, by the way. That's when my co-workers and friends started to avoid me. I thought they were jealous." She looked at Mason for a response. There was none. He had heard these stories before.

"One day, it was a Tuesday, I dropped one of the packages and it split open. Inside was money, a lot of money, betting slips, and papers with insider trading tips written on them." She tried to read Mason's face hoping she would not have to tell more.

"Were there any narcotics or delivery instructions in the package?"

"Not that I saw," Carla said.

"Go on," Mason urged.

"I realized what was going on. I had been taking part in illegal activities. Activities that may have hurt innocent people. I was gullible, not stupid." The memory was vivid. A chill ran down Carla's back. She began to shiver. Her lips trembled. Her hands began to shake. She clasped her hands together and placed them in her lap. She closed her eyes and counted to three, then continued.

"I confronted him. He became livid. His eyes narrowed. The veins on his head looked ready to burst. He pulled his lips tight over his clenched teeth. His forehead was taunt. He put his face right next to mine and yelled at me. He said I should have been more careful. He said I had no idea what I had done. Then he said since I had seen what was in the package, it made me part of the action. I was scared, so I backed off."

"That's not the whole story. What happened next?"

"I told him I was sorry. I said I overreacted. Then I fixed him a drink and rubbed his back and acted all sweet. He seemed to calm down. Everything seemed normal for a few days. So when he was sleeping, I went through his pockets and found his little black book. My worst fears were confirmed. His friends were in the mob."

"Which mob?" Mason had taken on a very stern look.

"I'm not sure exactly which family. It could have been the Stefanos or the Gracanos. It doesn't matter. Any mob is *The Mob*."

"Is that when he gave you the gun?"

Carla lowered her head and said softly, "No."

"You are going to tell me," Mason said with a demanding tone.

Carla looked up with tears ready to brim over. "Please don't tell anyone. No one here knows and I don't want to lose the friends I've made. And I don't want any of this getting back to New York. I believe there were bad people back there and I don't want to catch their attention."

"What happened, Carla?"

"Winston and I were walking past a jewelry store on our way to lunch. Suddenly he pushed me into the store and told me to pick out a bracelet. While I was looking for a bracelet, I noticed he kept looking out the front window. When I found one I liked, I took it to him at the window. There was a long black limousine driving slowly past the store. I didn't think anything of it at the time. The limousine windows were dark. The faces of the people in it were blurry. A few minutes later, we heard the shots. Winston told the clerk to put the bracelet on his tab, told me to go back to the office, and left. The newspapers reported the shooting as a rival mob hit against a mid-level dealer."

"If Winston was just delivering packages, he would be a mid-level dealer," Mason stated in a matter-of-fact way, watching for Carla's reaction. Carla leaned her head to the side and shrugged her shoulders. "Continue," Mason urged.

"The next day two men came to the office. Winston saw them coming down the hall and told me to go home. I thought we were going to have a special evening. When I went to work in the morning, Winston was anxious and agitated. The knot of his tie was pulled down three inches below the collar of his wrinkled shirt. His face was lined and his forehead was furrowed. Obviously, he had not slept. The other secretaries told me the two men questioned Winston about the shooting behind closed doors. They said it got quite loud, and when Winston came out, he was as pale as a ghost. That's when he gave me the gun."

"Did you ever shoot it?"

"No."

"What made you come to Otra Vez?"

"A few days after I found his little black book, we were at the apartment. Winston said he didn't want me to get hurt. So to protect me, he was going to buy out my employment contract. The buyout agreement included wording that said any and all activities undertaken during my employment were privileged, and if I divulged any information I would be prosecuted. I knew from the amount that it was not a buyout. It was hush money. I was scared and mixed up. I took the money and ran. I ended up here in Otra Vez."

Carla leaned forward and grasped Mason's hands. "Please don't tell anyone. No one knows. Please!"

"Why didn't you come forward with the information you had regarding the client scams, the packages, and the shooting?"

"Because it wouldn't do any good. It wasn't enough information to convict anyone. Some innocent people might be damaged. And none of the victims would be compensated. And, I know it's selfish, but my reputation would be ruined."

"What does this have to do with the incident at the Cliff House?" Mason was trying to understand Carla's thinking.

"When I came out of my office and saw everyone looking at the stairs, I knew something bad was going on. I heard sounds coming from the second-floor room. It is my employee Dirk Jenkins' room. Douglas, the scum-ball I shot, stays there when he spends the night. I guess my imagination took over.

"I walked up the stairs and stopped right outside the door of the room. I heard voices. A girl's and a man's. I recognized Sissy's, but not the man's. When I heard him say, 'You have everything Hollywood wants,' I knew it was Douglas and what he was doing. It was Winston all over again. I pushed open the door and told Sissy to meet me in my office. She is only seventeen, almost eighteen. And I told Douglas to get out. Then I went to my living quarters and called Gustav. I told him I wanted the room gutted. I do not want anything that Douglas may have touched in my house. He is evil!" Her voice started to shake. She paused to regain her composure. "I started back to Dirk's room where Douglas was. I was furious. I thought of the gun Winston had given me. That should have tipped me off about Winston. Young girls don't think that way. You know?"

Mason tilted his head to the side. He didn't agree, but thought it best not to say so.

"I picked up the gun. As I said, I had never fired it, didn't ever expect to. I never loaded it. I guess Winston did. Anyway, when I went back to the room and saw Douglas hadn't left, I became enraged. I told him again to leave. He started to talk in a condescending tone. I pulled the gun from my pocket. A noise or something startled me, and the gun went off. Douglas started to scream at me. It was very strange. Douglas sounded and looked just like Winston. I saw blood running down his arm. I heard another gun shot and Douglas was yelling for help. Everything after that is a blur, until I heard Ron's voice this morning. Ron said he would send you."

Mason leaned back in his chair. This was not what he expected. "Carla," he began slowly, "I need to do some research. I need to talk to some of the people that were there. You understand?"

"Yes. They will tell you what I did. Except the New York stuff. They don't know about that. Please don't tell them," Carla pleaded again.

Mason left and drove immediately to the Cliff House. Gustav and his crew were there demolishing the room. Phillip and his cooking staff were helping. Dirk was trying to. Mason introduced himself and everyone let loose. He heard the same story told with different words, some of which he had not heard since his younger days. A number of threats were directed at Douglas. Many offered to speak in Carla's defense, if the need arose. Finally, Phillip offered Mason a sandwich. They walked to the front porch, where the ocean view had a calming effect. Phillip told Mason his take on the event and promised to do anything to help. He told Mason he loved Carla. "Have you told her?" Mason asked. Phillip bit his lip and lowered his head.

Attorney James Mason left the Cliff House and drove straight to the hospital in Sea Port. Approaching Douglas's room, he could hear Douglas giving the nurse trouble. "No sense in trying to be nice to this guy." Over time Mason had learned how to deal with different personalities. He had enough experience with Hollywood personalities to know egos were their driving force and everything was about the show. He stopped and put on his necktie and jacket.

Entering Douglas's room, he introduced himself and quickly added that he was Carla DuPree's attorney.

"Well you can tell that bitch she is about to lose everything," Douglas's voice echoed through the hall.

"Mr. Douglas, I have advised my client not to tell anyone you were in the process of raping a minor when she stopped you."

"What? I didn't rape the... What do you mean, minor?"

"The girl is only seventeen."

"Why was she working there?"

"She needed money. She was of legal age to work in a restaurant."

Douglas paused and then continued, "I wasn't trying to rape her. Hell, I didn't even get all her clothes off her."

"Although you did try," Mason finished the thought.

"That's no reason for Carla to shoot me. Twice, I might add."

"Carla prevented you from committing a crime that would put you in jail for many years. Your leg and shoulder will heal quickly, unless you are in jail. There they might become infected. Jail is not the cleanest place, you know. Tell you what, you agree not to press charges, and I'll get Carla to agree not to tell the newspapers what happened."

"Newspapers!"

"Newspapers—*The L.A. Times*, *The Enquirer*—do you have another publication in mind?"

"That would ruin me."

Mason concurred. "Sign this paper and I will take it directly to Carla. The matter will be settled this afternoon."

Douglas snapped the paper out of Mason's hands and scribbled his signature at the bottom. Mason reached out his hand to shake with Douglas. Douglas turned away. Mason snickered and headed back to Otra Vez.

Attorney James Mason was feeling smug about stopping Douglas from suing Carla. Still, there was a potential criminal case. He needed to meet with the sheriff to determine his next course of action.

When Mason arrived at the Otra Vez jail, the sheriff was sitting outside. His eyes were red and his nose looked sore. The sheriff acknowledged Mason with a tilt of his head. "What happened to you?" Mason asked.

The sheriff pointed to the door of the jail and said, "See for yourself."

Mason walked in. The place was full of flowers—bouquets, potted plants, arrangements—all in full bloom. The air was thick with pollen. Mason made his way through the flowers to Carla's cell. Carla was sniffling too. He explained the paper Douglas had signed. She signed it immediately. "I still have to talk to the sheriff about any action the town may take," He reminded her.

"I appreciate everything you are doing," Carla said with misty eyes. Mason didn't know if it was tears or allergies.

"Where'd all those flowers come from?" Mason asked the sheriff while blowing his nose.

"Practically everyone in town," the sheriff sniffed. "She's a popular girl around here."

"I talked with Douglas. He has signed a paper agreeing not to file charges. What about the city? Will they be charging Carla?"

The sheriff leaned back in his chair. "The way I see it, Douglas was trespassing. She had told him to get out. He didn't. He had threatened Sissy, Carla's employee, and therefore, by extension, Carla. It was self-defense. Since you have the paper signed by Douglas, as soon as I can fill out the release form, she is free to go."

"The flowers are a problem, aren't they?"

"Yes, they are."

"How about I take them to the Cliff House so you can go back inside?"

"I'll be mighty grateful."

Mason called the Cliff House. Dirk was more than happy to have a job to do and hurried to his car as soon as Mason hung up. The flowers were gone, the release was signed, and Carla was walking out of the jail with Mason when Ron Gunderson arrived. "It's all over," Carla shouted triumphantly.

"I missed it?" Ron exclaimed. Carla nodded. Mason reached out his hand and introduced himself to Ron. "Thank you," Ron said. "You have no idea what this means to me."

"I think I have a pretty good idea. She's quite a girl."

Carla blushed. "This calls for a special dinner."

"You should go to the best place in town," the sheriff advised.

"Where?" Mason and Ron asked in unison.

"My place, of course!" Carla said proudly, pointing both her thumbs at herself.

They had a sumptuous lobster and steak dinner prepared by Phillip himself and served by Sissy under Dirk's watchful eye. Afterwards, Mason walked the grounds, admiring the gardens and views. Ron and Carla sat on the front porch steps talking. Ron brought Carla up to date on the New York scene, and she told him the history of the Cliff House. When they ran out of small talk, Carla looked straight into Ron's eyes. "Ron," she said, "I'm not sorry."

Ron grew tense. "What are you talking about?" he asked with trepidation.

"Shooting Douglas. I'm not sorry. My mind must have played tricks on me. It was like I was facing Winston all over again. I just lost it. I've wanted to get Winston for a long time. And it feels to me like I have. At least I got someone like him. They're all the same." She turned and looked at Ron's eyes.

"It's over Carla. You can move on now." Ron put his arm around her shoulder and she leaned against him. But she did not cry.

Ron and Mason left by way of the Pacific Coast Highway. Neither one wanted to drive the Otra Vez road after dark. Carla threw kisses and hugs as they left.

"Ron is right," she thought. "The barn-theater remodeling is moving along. Gustav has started gutting the 'crime scene.' I can move forward." She headed to the crime scene to check on the progress. It was a mess. A big pile of rubble was in the center of the room. She noticed the closet had not been touched. "I will speak with Gustav first thing in the morning."

CHAPTER TWENTY-EIGHT

The Box

Carla slept late the day after her time in jail. At least, she intended to sleep late. The sound of demolition woke her. She put the pillow over her head. It didn't help. Giving up, she crawled out of bed and dragged herself to the mirror. She wished she hadn't.

She pulled on a pair of jeans, added a plaid blouse, slipped on a pair of sandals, and fluffed her hair. "That will do for a while," she comforted herself.

On the way downstairs, she stopped at the "crime scene" room being remodeled. Gustav came over the second he saw her. "I'm glad to see you," he said, smiling broadly. "The room is coming along nicely. We should be done gutting it today. Gertie is coming by later to see about the remodeling and decorating. Wanda said to tell you she's only a phone call away when you need her."

Carla's ears perked up. Hoping Gustav was spending more time with Wanda, she asked, "You talked to Wanda? How is she?"

"She's fine," Gustav said sheepishly. Carla smiled.

"You are going to remove that closet, aren't you?" Carla more demanded than asked.

"That's a good-size closet. It can hold a lot on the top shelf in addition to hanging clothes," Gustav gently argued.

"It's obviously not original to the house. Neither the crown molding nor the baseboard is dovetailed at the walls. And the floor boards run straight through. I want it out."

"I can do that," Gustav mumbled, shaking his head at how wasteful it was. Everyone needs a closet eventually.

"I appreciate you doing this so promptly. I hope it hasn't caused you any problems with your other clients."

"Miss Carla, my other clients have offered to help. It was a terrible thing that man tried to do to our Sissy. We are all in your debt for standing up to him. I hope it won't hurt your theater project."

"Keeping that scum-bag around would have hurt the theater project and the Cliff House. I'm glad we caught him when we did. Heaven only knows what damage he could have done. Dirk is really the one working the theater project anyway. Have you seen him?"

"He was in the barn last time I saw him. He's been sleeping there."

"Oh no! We'll have to get one of the other rooms ready for him until this one is finished. I'll talk to him."

Carla went to the kitchen and got some toast with coffee. Her head was beginning to clear when Gertie, her friend and decorator, arrived. "Pull up a chair, Gertie, and have a cup of coffee."

Gertie gave Carla a thorough look-over. "You look pretty good for an ex-con," she teased.

Carla laughed. "I wasn't there long, but let me tell you, I don't want to go back." Changing the subject, she added, "Have you seen the room?"

"I saw it before. And I checked it out again yesterday, after the yellow tape was removed. It's a very large room. I think it would make two nice-size rooms. We could put a bath at the end of the hall-way and then you would have six rooms to rent out once the front four are redone."

"I can see the two rooms. I'm not so sure about the shared bath. I think most hotels are doing a bath for each room now."

"People have gotten spoiled since the war ended. And waste-ful," Gertie observed.

Silence fell over the Cliff House. Carla looked at Gertie. Gertie's eyes got big. "What happened? Why did the work stop?" Gertie whispered.

Carla felt dread creeping up her spine. Both women rose and slowly walked down the hallway to the bottom of the stairs. They heard muffled talking among the demolition workers. "What are they saying?" Gertie asked in a hushed voice.

"I can't understand them," Carla said softly.

Jimmy came running down the stairs. "I must get Mr. Gustav," he shouted and hurried out the back door.

A few minutes later he came back with Gustav. Gustav was growling, "This better be good."

Jimmy and Gustav nodded their heads in greetings to the women and continued upstairs. Carla and Gertie glanced at each other, then followed quickly.

When the workers began knocking down the clothes closet, they found an unusual-looking box. It was ten inches long at most and probably less than six inches wide. There were no hinges, no lock, and no obvious way of opening it. A shiny black lacquer finish covered the box, and gold dragons were painted on the sides. In between the dragons were gold vines with red roses. More red roses and vines were painted on the top. Curved legs, about three-quarters of an inch long, were on each corner.

Gustav brought the box over to Carla. "I don't think it's worth much, but it is pretty," he offered by way of explanation.

"It's very mysterious," Gertie added.

"Can you open it?" Carla asked.

"I don't see any way. And I don't want to break it trying," Gustav, always cautious, admitted.

Carla took the box. It felt very light. She gently shook it. Something moved inside. She looked over it carefully. It was pretty, but not very big. Gustav was right, it did not look or feel expensive. "It could be a jewelry box," she suggested. "I know! We'll have a contest. Whoever guesses what's in the box gets a free meal."

"Make it two," Gertie shouted, catching the excitement of the moment.

"Make it a dinner for four!" Carla called back. The workers immediately started making wild guesses: diamonds, rubies, gold nuggets. They about doubled over laughing at each other. Everyone wanted to eat at the Cliff House.

Dirk walked in, "What's so funny?" Carla showed him the box and told him the plan. "That's a fantastic idea. We can hold the great reveal when the room is finished. It will be really good publicity for the Cliff House and the theater." Carla and Dirk went to her office to make plans for the contest. Gertie stayed and took measurements of the room.

Carla hung posters advertising the "Mystery Box Contest" in the hardware store, jewelry store, beauty shop, and at Garcia's Gardens. Word spread rapidly, like all news in Otra Vez. People started guessing immediately. The picnic basket Carla fixed to hold the guesses filled in no time. She added a second picnic basket. Business was booming. The barn-theater, now known as Dirk's Theater, was taking shape. Carla and Gertie were in the final stages of decorating the rooms when Dirk ran in carrying a dirty dilapidated cardboard box. "Look!" he shouted, although no one was more than three feet away.

He sat the box in the middle of the room. Everyone gathered around. Dirk was in such a hurry, he accidentally tore one top flap off the box. Gasps, oohs, and ahhs filled the room. The box was full of pictures. Some were in the Ansel Adams style, some were line drawings, some appeared to be water colors. Most were of the Cliff House trees and gardens in the late 1800s. "I need to get these framed," Carla cried with delight. "They belong in the Starburst room."

"The ones of the trees belong in this room. You can see them from this window," Gertie babbled excitedly as she reached for more. "What are you going to name these rooms anyway?"

Carla hadn't really thought about it. "I guess we'll call one The Mystery Box and the other we'll name after the winner of the contest."

Gertie did not approve. "How about the Big Tree Room? These pictures would be perfect for that," she offered.

"Of course," Carla giggled. A new idea was forming in her mind. With all these historical pictures, perhaps they could do an art show. She would talk to Dirk about it.

CHAPTER TWENTY-NINE

Time Is Short

It was Wednesday morning. Carla had called a meeting to finalize the plans for the Mystery Box Contest finale. The contest end date was only ten days away. Since the weather was balmy, the meeting was held on the front porch overlooking the peaceful ocean. Dirk reported the theater would be complete enough to give the visitors a preview of what was in store. Phillip was still working on menus. He was considering both fancy and plain. Gustav said the room where the Mystery Box was found was ready for visitors. Gertie believed the found garden pictures would be framed and ready to hang in a few days.

"What do you think of using those pictures as an historic art show?" Carla suggested enthusiastically. Gertie's face turned to stone.

Dirk spoke up, "That would be a good idea, but not at the same time as the contest finale. The pictures wouldn't get the attention they deserve. Besides, an art show could be another special event to attract another crowd." Carla hadn't thought of that.

Gertie relaxed. "I agree. People are going to be interested in winning a free dinner, not looking at art."

Carla was still considering their comments when a car was heard pulling into the parking lot. "It's too early for guests," she murmured.

A young woman about five-foot-five, wearing a white silk blouse with a sailor collar outlined with red and blue ribbons, and white wide-leg slacks, walked toward them. Her hair was blond and cut to her shoulders. Every strand was in place. Her makeup was perfect, not too heavy. Dirk stood up knocking over his chair. "Sally Sailor!" he screamed and ran to her.

Bewildered, the others looked at each other. No one said anything. They all kept their eyes focused on Dirk. "How long do you have? Gee, you look great. I was afraid to hope you would actually come here. Boy, I'm glad you're here." The kiss they shared was not a happy-to-see-an-old-co-worker kiss. "Hey, everyone, this is Sally Sailor. She was a concierge and entertainer on the ship. Gosh, it's good to see you."

"Welcome." "Hi." "Glad you're here." The group stumbled over their words.

Carla reached out and, taking Sally by the hand, led her to a chair. "So you know Dirk." It sounded brainless even to Carla.

Sally gave a captivating smile. "Yes. We met on the ship, but fraternizing with the crew was strictly forbidden. So we couldn't be open about our feelings. He's a great guy," she said turning and leaning on Dirk's chest.

"I'm so glad to see you," Dirk said again, wrapping his arms around her. "I hope you can stay. We're having a big to-do here next week. I hope you can stay. When did you dock?"

"The ship docked two days ago. My contract is up so it took me a while to clear ship."

"You're out?" Dirk couldn't hide his excitement. He picked Sally up and swung her around.

Phillip did not look happy. It was obvious now. Dirk never intended to make a play for Carla. "Why didn't you tell us about Sally?" he mumbled.

"I told you I wouldn't compete with you," Dirk smirked.

"You could have told me why," Phillip snapped.

"It was too much fun watching you try to match my time," Dirk teased.

"Cheese blintzes for everyone except Dirk," Phillip snapped, more angry with himself than Dirk. The little group's snickers broke into uncontrolled laughter.

"Let me help you," Carla said and followed Phillip into the house. She watched him slam the refrigerator door shut and push the dishes on the counter out of his way.

Carla and Phillip had a business arrangement. He prepared the menus and supplied the cooks and waiters. She paid the wages for the staff. Phillip was supposed to bill her for his time. So far he hadn't. The deal had worked out well for both sides. The Cliff House clientele was increasing and his cooking school was prospering thanks to the internships and additional classes teaching sophisticated dishes. Lately though, Carla had come to realize she wanted his friendship more. No, that wasn't exactly true. What she wanted from him was way more than friendship, and it had nothing to do with the Cliff House.

With a hesitant voice, she asked, "What did Dirk mean when he said he wouldn't compete with you? Compete how?" She wasn't sure she wanted to know. "Were you competing to see who could take over the Cliff House?" Carla asked with her heart in her throat.

Phillip's mouth dropped open. His nose wrinkled. His eyebrows were pulled down and his eyes were squinched. "No! No! Why would you say such a thing?" Phillip was shaken. He wanted to tell her how he rearranged his entire schedule so he could take her places to keep her away from Dirk. He wanted to tell her why he spent way more time here than necessary to prepare menus trying to keep her away from Dirk. He would have been concentrating on wooing her rather than beating Dirk's time, if he had known about Sally. "It has nothing to do with the Cliff House." He took a deep breath to gather his courage. "It's all about …"

"Carla," Wanda yelled as she hurried down the hall to the kitchen. "Carla, the plans for the big Mystery Box Finale are amazing. I can hardly wait." She stopped short when she saw Carla's and Phillip's faces. "Whoops. Looks like my timing is bad. Sorry if I interrupted something. I'll leave now." Wanda turned to leave.

"Wait, Wanda," Carla said as she grabbed a tray of cheese blintzes. "These blintzes are ready to serve."

Phillip stood still with his heart pounding. "I wish I had at least a drop of Dirk's bravado with women," he mumbled.

Another car pulled up. It was Sammy from the antique shop, with some antique frames perfect for the found tree and garden pictures. Gertie matched them up immediately.

Time was running short and there was still lots to do for the Mystery Box Finale.

CHAPTER THIRTY

Finally

On the day of the Mystery Box Finale, guests began arriving at noon, even though the opening was not scheduled till six o'clock. Wanda, Gustav, and Gertie were among the first. Many more people than expected turned out. Phillip called in two more student cooks and waiters and added a picnic lunch served in a paper bag to the menu. Since the crowd was so large, and the sky was clear with a gentle breeze and white puffy clouds, it was decided to hold the event on the front porch overlooking the calm, blue Pacific Ocean.

The black lacquer Mystery Box with the dragons and red roses was brought to the center of the steps leading off the front porch. Old man Garcia had not seen it until now. No one noticed his face growing pale or his gait becoming wobbly as he inched his way to the back of the crowd.

Dirk raised his hands to get everyone's attention and signaled to be quiet. "My good friend, Sally Sailor, will start us off with a special song she has written especially for this occasion." The crowd cheered.

Sally started singing, *"We are glad to greet you, we are glad you're here."* The crowd began cheering again so loud the rest of the song was lost.

"After the contest winner is named, Sally will sing again for you at the pre-opening show at Dirk's Theater." Dirk was in his glory. "And," he continued, "Sissy will be joining her." With that news, the crowd erupted with shouts and cheers. Everyone loves their home-town talent. Dirk stepped to the side and motioned for Carla to come forward. "And now the moment you have been waiting for!" Carla, dressed in a long pink flowered sundress with small cap sleeves, a necklace made of seashells, and white sandals, stepped forward and bowed.

She walked to the first picnic basket full of guesses and reached in. Before she could pick an entry, a long black limousine spun into the parking lot, throwing gravel everywhere. The guests all turned to look. Carla turned pale. A pit formed in her stomach. Her smile disappeared. Thoughts raced through her mind. "New York must have heard about the shooting. They came to ruin me. They won't. I have friends here, real friends."

She turned to Dirk. "Is the sheriff here?"

"Why?"

"I may need him."

"Where's the gun, Carla?"

"The sheriff kept it. Said he wouldn't give it back till I learned how to shoot it properly."

Dirk breathed a sigh of relief. "He's here. Everyone is here."

The driver helped an older man dressed in a striped double-breasted suit into a wheelchair and was pushing as fast as he could while the older man barked orders on where to go. Some people recognized the older man and quickly whispered to others. "It's Richardson."

Mr. Richardson passed within three feet of Garcia and did not acknowledge him. Garcia's eyes narrowed. He stood tall. His fists clenched. Juan hurried to his side. "Please, Mr. Garcia, don't let that man ruin the good reputation you have earned."

Garcia's breathing was fast and deep. He turned to Juan, "Don't worry, Juan." But Juan was worried. He was not the only one, the whole town had much to lose if anything happened to Garcia.

Carla began pulling a guess from the picnic basket. "I will pay you $20,000 for that box," Richardson shouted. "That's five years' salary." He stopped just short of adding "for someone like you." But Carla knew what he meant. She looked him directly in the eye. Pulling her forehead down, she squinted at him. Something about him was familiar. Although she tried, she couldn't put her finger on what it was.

Phillip eased his way beside her and whispered, "That is Richardson, the park statue." Carla understood. Richardson had sent his daughter, Anna, to the Nuns' Home for Unwed Mothers at the Cliff House to have her baby. Somehow he knew about the Box and now wanted to claim it. Probably to stop gossip or the truth. She wasn't sure which.

Carla's eyes never left Richardson. She watched as he reached down and rubbed his right shin. Remembering kicking the same leg on the statue, she did her best to hide her smirk. "Mr. Richardson, we are in the middle of a contest. Everyone here has submitted an entry to win. Did you submit an entry?"

"No. I will pay you $25,000," he offered desperately.

"Mr. Richardson, if I was to sell you the Mystery Box, I would have to cancel my contest. All these fine people would think I was a fraud. My reputation would be ruined. Let me tell you, Mr. Richardson, I will not sell my reputation for any amount of money." To herself she added, "ever again."

The crowd cheered. Garcia gave her a thumbs up. No one had ever dared to speak to Mr. Richardson in that manner.

Dirk stepped forward, "Let the contest go on!" he shouted.

Carla began reading the entries. Gold coins was a favorite and guessed many times. Jewelry, treasure map, love letters, and dead flowers were next in popularity. There was one guess for a tin whistle, one for sea shells, and two for nothing. It took over an hour to read all the entries. Finally, it was time to open the Mystery Box. Everyone had studied the box. No one could figure out how to open it. So it was decided to use a gold-painted screw driver and a hammer with a red ribbon tied on the handle to force the top off. Hopefully, they wouldn't destroy the whole thing.

When Garcia saw what was planned, he yelled, "Stop!" Flabbergasted, everyone turned and looked at him. Most had never heard him speak. And no one had ever heard him yell. He took a deep breath and, trying not to seem too interested, said, "It is a Chinese magic box. They used to give them as prizes for knocking over milk bottles at the arcade games on the beach." He stopped. Had he given away too much? What if he was wrong? With Richardson showing up, he was sure he was right. Still, there was a chance he was wrong. "You pull gently down on one of the legs and turn it."

"You do it," Carla said, holding out the Mystery Box.

"No, you can do it," Garcia answered quickly. He didn't want anyone to see how badly his hands were shaking.

Carla pulled gently on the front right leg. Sure enough it popped down about a quarter inch. She smiled. Cheers rose from the crowd. Carla turned the leg. The top swiveled in the direction of the turn and revealed a photograph. Carla held the picture for all to see.

A hush fell over the crowd. Whispers began circulating. Was this a hoax? Was it just an advertising scheme? Did Richardson put Carla up to this? What was he trying to prove?

Tears filled Garcia's eyes. He was right. It was the box he had won for Anna right before her father, Mr. Richardson, sent him away. She had Garcia's baby at the former Nuns' Home for Unwed Mothers, now the Cliff House. She must have hidden the box to protect its contents. She never would have accidently left it there.

Carla looked at Phillip. "What's going on?"

"Carla," Phillip began, gently putting his hand on her back. "That is a picture of you."

"It can't be. It's at least thirty years old." Suddenly Carla understood. She had been adopted thirty years ago. Hurriedly she rifled through the rest of the contents until she found another picture— one of her mother with her father. She looked at Garcia accusingly. "You knew," she spat.

All eyes turned to Garcia, the man everyone respected. The man who had helped all of them one way or another. "I knew the minute I saw you. But I had no proof. The records were sealed. But I knew you were Anna's daughter, my daughter. I don't know what brought you here…" He choked up.

Carla didn't know what to say. Stunned, she simply stood there on the porch speechless. The crowd began shaking Garcia's hands and patting him on the back, congratulating him on having a wonderful daughter. He smiled and thanked them, but never took his eyes off Carla. No one spoke to Richardson. His wheelchair was blocked. He couldn't get away.

"Cake for everyone," Phillip announced. His answer was always to feed people.

"The pre-opening show of the Dirk Theater will begin in fifteen minutes," Dirk called out over the din.

When the crowd had wandered off, Garcia approached Richardson. "How could you not know Carla was Anna's daughter? Didn't you see how her mouth curls up on the right side when she smiles? Just like Anna's. Didn't you see how confident and deliberate she walks? Didn't you see her beautiful eyes with long lashes, or notice her long slender fingers? She plays the piano, just like Anna, you know." Richardson turned away from him. Garcia's anger flared. He grabbed Richardson by the throat with his rough workman's hands. "What happened to the letters I sent to Anna?" he demanded.

"I destroyed them. I told her that when you found out she was pregnant, you left town."

Garcia pushed Richardson's head back. "You robbed me of the joy of watching my child grow up. And you robbed yourself of your daughter and your granddaughter. You're not worthy of my anger, and I will not reduce myself to your level to get even." Garcia let go of Richardson's head and walked away. Richardson's head dropped forward. Tears dropped from his cheeks to his chest. His chauffeur pushed his wheelchair to the car. They left unnoticed while the other guests were enjoying the show at Dirk's Theater.

The pre-opening musical at Dirk's Theater was spectacular. The audience gave Sally and Sissy a standing ovation. Their cheering and shouting continued clear to the parking lot as the audience headed home.

Phillip drove his students home and went directly to his red brick house on the side of the hill across from Garcia's. There he would be able to see the lights come on at Garcia's house. While he paced back and forth gathering his courage, he practiced the words he intended to use.

When the evening's activities wound down and quiet had settled over the Cliff House, Garcia approached Carla. He took her hands and, looking directly in her eyes, said, "Of all the girls in this world that may have been my daughter, I'm glad it is you."

Carla blushed. "How many bottles did you have to knock down to win the Box?" she asked.

"Thousands. My arm still hurts when it rains," Garcia chuckled while rubbing his arms at the memory.

"We have a lot of catching up to do," Carla responded gently. "I want to know about my mother."

"And I want to know about the folks who raised you. I want to know everything you did." They sat on the porch a while longer just being together. It was their Otra Vez, another time, a second chance.

185

Phillip was waiting impatiently on his patio watching Garcia's house. As soon as the first light appeared, Phillip was in his car headed to Carla. His words were ready. His chest was puffed up with bravado. Tonight, he would tell Carla he had loved her ever since that night on the beach, and would love her forevermore.

EPILOGUE

The events at the Cliff House's Mystery Box Finale, including the eye-opening revelations, were the talk of Otra Vez for quite a while. Carla had made her way into not only the pocketbooks of the entire community, but also their hearts. Gossip about who was doing what, and what Carla would be doing next, kept the little town buzzing.

The possibility of an incline like Pittsburgh's or a cable car like San Francisco's reaching from the cove to the top of the cliff had both the businesses and citizens humming. Not only would it be practical; it would also be a tourist attraction. The taxi service was particularly interested in both ideas. They wanted to be in charge.

Ships can still be seen coming and going to China. The redwoods have grown taller. The sun continues to shine and young couples continue to meet and play on the beautiful, clean, sandy beach. Occasionally, the ghost is still mentioned, sometimes seen, and each time invariably ends with a trip to Carla's Cliff House.